LEONIE HENDRICKS: DEMON P.I.

(A WORLD OF NAVA KATZ NOVEL)

DEBORAH WILDE

te da media
vancouver

Book Layout ©2015 BookDesignTemplates.com

Cover design by Damonza

Issued in print and electronic formats.

ISBN 978-1-988681-24-5 (paperback)

ISBN 978-1-988681-26-9 (EPUB)

ISBN 978-1-988681-25-2 (Kindle)

ISBN: 978-1-988681-34-4 (Large Print Edition)

1

"He loves me." *Pluck.*

The asper demon flinched and thrashed against his binding, as I ripped another one of his tiny wings off his knobby shoulder. It was less like wishing on a four-leaf clover and more like plucking a cantankerous, still-living chicken.

The bits of him that weren't chained to the wall with solid iron cuffs were pinned using iron knives like a butterfly specimen, while his three eyes were nothing more than puffy lumps in an already lumpy face from the concentrated salt and ghost pepper spray that I'd subdued him with. And sure, this sounded serial killer sadistic, but aspers were notorious for disemboweling first and asking questions later.

"He loves me not." *Pluck.*

"Suck it, sweetheart." The demon shook his rattlesnake tail at me, his sneer growing lewder.

Using one of the many blades casually tossed on the table next to me, I impaled his penis stand-in.

He screamed, a high-pitched buzzing cry.

"Next time, get consent to bring that swizzle stick of yours to show-and-tell." I kicked aside the pile of wings that resembled strips of dried jerky scattered at my feet. The friendly chat I'd called him in for had now gone on about three hours too long. Time to get what I needed and have a snack.

"Daeva's horn. You have it. Where'd it go?" I twisted the blade in deeper, taking no perverse thrills in this single-minded violence. My mentor and boss, Harry Dunn, had pounded it into me to never apply a human moral code where demons were concerned. My life was on the line with every single interaction, and power was the only language demons responded to. I'd become fluent, even if I always attempted to negotiate my way out first.

"She took from me. I took from her." The asper spat blood at me, hitting me square in the face. There it was, the "an eye for an eye" philosophy these thuggish demons employed. Actually, it was more, "an eye for you looked at me funny," or "an eye for, well, it's Tuesday," with these guys.

I was going to take things up a notch when a few drops of asper blood got in my mouth and my inner goblin awoke with a vengeance, clawing for supremacy. The blood was hot and rich, with just an edge of savory. My fingers froze into claw forma-tions, my half-demon side howling in my head and forming a dark shadow in the white light that I always imagined my human body suffused with.

I eyed the asper like he was a chicken and I was the Colonel.

Wiping the blood off my tongue with my sleeve, I spun around and shouldered out the door, tossing my heavy gloves on the ground. Sweat ran down my neck into my protective suit.

"You're getting demon all over my nice office." Harry jabbed a bony finger at the gloves, causing the unlit cigarette hanging off the bottom left corner of his mouth to quiver. "Keep that mess in the interrogation room."

I stumbled past him into the small kitchen here at Dunn and Associates P.I.—a misnomer if there was one, as there was only one Associate and right now she was scrabbling at the cupboard, teetering on the balls of her feet, balance shot. I was so, so hungry.

Harry found me a protein bar, unwrapping it and shoving it at me in record time. "Je nourris. Tu nourris. Say it, Leo."

"Je nourris. Tu–" I shuddered, a red wash coloring my vision.

My phone rang, buzzing against my thigh.

Harry grasped my chin and forced me to look him in the eyes. "Chew and talk, kiddo."

"Nourris. Elle nourrit. I feed. You feed. She feeds." I repeated the mantra that he and I had come up with to remind myself that where and how I fed was a choice. That my human nature was still in control. Had I caved to my demon half, blood sustenance would no longer be optional. Blood was life to goblins, it was sacred, and to refuse it, like I did, was blasphemy.

And friends wondered why I never had any interest in vampire stories. It wasn't so sexy when you lived it day in and day out.

Six more times my phone rang, but I couldn't answer, fighting to firmly reassert my human side. Despite my determination to eat from the basic food groups and not someone's bleeding heart, I still had to chow down more often than most people. Luckily, I metabolized faster as well, so by the time I'd scarfed back an entire bag of chocolate-covered almonds, the haze and the frenzied need had faded.

Classical music floated in from the front office. Ugh. Mahler.

My phone rang yet again. Seven missed calls–all from my mother. She wouldn't stop until I answered. *Please let someone be dead.* "Hey, Mom."

"Lord protect us. I just had the television on and they were reporting fresh demons on the prowl in Vancouver. Fresh! As if they were ripe melons. I was so worried about you, and then when I couldn't reach you, I feared the worst. Leonie, you need to come to church and pray. It's the only way we're going to survive this plague of evil. That's what we get for our sinful ways."

Pretty damn ironic, since she'd had the one-night stand with my goblin sire, believing him nothing more than a charming and very human rogue, and I was the one suffering the consequences.

Gripping the edge of the counter, I tried to tune out her distressed chatter, wishing I could yell that her every word hit me like a bullet. Or just snap and show her the reds of my eyes, rip the veil off her world once and for all. But I'd never do that. I was a good daughter, the child who understood her fears. Not one more part of the nightmare.

"Which church is it this week?" I said. "Baptist? Evangelical? You've gone through so many since demons came out." What little patience I had for her constant doom and gloom had been worn thin in tamping down my blood rush.

Harry snatched the phone away, calming her down with some bullshit until he managed to end the call, while I stewed at my outburst with petty satisfaction and a heap of guilt.

My mood felt reflected in the ugly décor. The kitchen walls were covered in hideous blue tiles printed with gold horseshoes left over from the short-lived business before us that sold bogus timeshares in Vegas, but the "wood grain" laminate counter boasted a top-of-the-line espresso maker so most days I counted the room a win.

Today, I counted it a lifeline. One quick cup to sharpen my wits then I'd wrap up this business with the asper. I slid a small ceramic cup under the stainless-steel nozzle and hit the button for a double shot, taking deep breaths in time to the rumbling of the machine.

Harry leaned back against the counter, his bushy white hair sticking up every which way. "She's a crackpot, but she means well. Some people just aren't equipped to handle the truth. Don't let her get to you."

"Helpful advice from a man who has yet to tell his mom he smokes."

"Don't piss me off or I'll replace you," he said.

4

"No, you won't," I said, "because if you fire me you'd have to change the sign, and you're way too cheap for that."

Technically, I was not yet licensed to be a private investigator and the scope of my duties should have been pretty limited. Realistically, we were dealing with demons. Who was going to file a complaint that I'd overstepped? I was Harry's right-hand woman, out in the field while he worked the desk after an altercation with a client that had left Harry hospitalized with three broken ribs and a shattered jaw a year ago. It wasn't always easy between us, but there was no one else I'd rather work for and no other place in Vancouver felt this much like home.

I hugged him. "I'm sorry."

"Mouthy youngster." He stole my espresso and slugged it back.

I got another espresso cup and tried a second time to caffeinate up. "Why the Mahler?"

Some people's moods could be read by their body language or clothing. For Harry it was his choice of classical music, and Mahler meant he was on edge.

"Nothing." Harry stuffed my phone in his pocket.

"Give it." I shot the espresso back.

"No. Break's over. Get back to work. Your do-gooder friends have cost me most of my business. Don't lose me the few clients we still have. No job left unresolved."

Harry's unbreakable rule that he'd drummed into me. Rules were important. They provided structure and an anchor to cling to when the world felt scarily awry.

"Demons are high off being outed to the public right now, so yeah, inter-demon business is slow," I said. "They're too busy terrifying the general population for the cameras, but it's a temporary blip and you know it. Another few weeks and they'll be coming to us with all their disputes. Meantime, considering we're being paid on an hourly rate, I'd think you'd show a little appreciation for my initiative in drawing out the billable hours."

Harry removed the cigarette from his mouth and stuffed it

behind his ear, dislodging the one already there. "Find out where the asper stashed the horn. The daeva promised a bonus if the horn was back within the week. And we like bonuses."

Bonuses were good, answers were better.

I stomped back to the interrogation room and kicked the door open, which thudded against the wall with a satisfying shudder. Cautiously, I stood at the threshold and inhaled, but my inner goblin didn't resurface. Stained concrete floor, rickety table with torture instruments placed at just the perfect angle to catch the cold glint of fluorescents, a scarred wooden wall, textured by years of thrashing spawn parts—the feng shui in here really pumped out those calming vibes.

Let's see. The nice cop routine hadn't worked. Offering to get back what the daeva had stolen from the asper hadn't worked. Torture hadn't worked. That left me with only one option.

"You're free to go." I pulled all the knives out, careful to only touch them by their carved wooden handles, and set them aside to be cleaned. As a half-demon, salt was no problem for me and even small doses of iron were okay, but long exposure, frequent handling, or just too much of the damn stuff, and I became severely weakened. Home Depot jaunts, fun as they were, required a shit-load of fortification and usually made me break out in hives.

Checking that the salt and ghost pepper spray was within reach, I retrieved a set of keys from my pocket and uncuffed the demon.

The asper slid to the floor on wobbly legs before catching himself. "Wrong move," he said and lunged for me.

I sidestepped him and held up a finger. "One sec."

Shocked, he actually froze, his right hand gripping his left forearm.

I snapped a photo of him on my phone, before typing in a quick text. "I'll just send this, shall I?"

"What's that?" His barbed unibrow kind of dipped in the middle which I figured was his way of frowning. He rubbed his slender forearm that draped down to the floor like a gorilla's. Was he fluffing it to get muscly and hard? Man, demons were weird.

"Just sending a quick text to Malik to let him know that there's going to be some blowback from the daeva. It's a small courtesy, but he likes to take an interest," I said.

"Like you know Malik." The asper sneered at me, but his lacerated rattlesnake tail vibrated wildly, indicative of distress. He continued to rub his left arm. Hmm. He hadn't been cuffed there, I hadn't stabbed him in that part of his arm, and his right forearm wasn't getting the same treatment.

"Personally, I've only met the demon king once." When the asshole had compelled me to use as a bargaining chip. Once was more than enough, thanks. "But my best friend Nava Katz was the one who helped him claim the throne. You've heard of her, right?"

The witch who had killed the demon who'd previously held the title of Satan and crowned a new King of Hell. The demons weren't sure if she was an ally or an enemy. A lot of the witches and Rasha, the male demon hunters, weren't either.

His eyes bugged out, or rather, they slurped through his swollen lids. He gulped. "Your best friend?"

"Yup. I'm tight with her Rasha boyfriend, too. And the witches. Huh. Might get pretty busy for you soon, just saying." I held up the phone. "So, the text? Sending, not sending?"

His rattle drooped. "You don't gotta get Malik or nobody involved."

"It's no trouble." I lowered my finger to the send button.

"No!"

I raised an eyebrow.

"I buried the horn," he said.

"Be more specific."

He went into great detail about the spit of land out on Annacis Island and the two trees next to a worn picnic table on the south end by a half-rotted log. All I had to do was measure out six paces from the end of the log pointing at the water and dig.

"Was that so hard?" I patted him on the arm he'd been rubbing, but he jerked away.

Oh no you don't, you big liar. I grabbed his forearm and using my redcap goblin magic, split his skin open. Black clotted liquid gushed out. Since redcaps fed off blood, they could suck it out hard enough to tear open flesh, dragging the innards out. Using my magic, even to draw blood didn't awaken my half-demon side. I'd decided it was because it was my magic and I was in control. It wasn't a skill set I was necessarily putting on my resume, but at times like this, it came in handy.

The asper jabbed at me with his rattle, but my magic was literally deflating him, compromising his ability to move, and I kept out of harm's way.

Gritting my teeth, I pulled harder. A jagged shard of bone punched up through the flesh.

He clubbed me across the side of my head with his free hand.

My hearing morphed into a ringing noise that throbbed through my brain. I adjusted my grip, probing and casting my awareness through his forearm until I hit some kind of blockage just before his wrist. I rent his flesh open from elbow to palm, focused on doing this efficiently and expediently, with as little pain as possible to the asper. Even if that asshole thought I'd fall for his lies, just because I was half-human.

The open flesh revealed a six-inch daeva horn embedded in his muscle.

The asper swung for me again, but I'd disoriented him enough that his motion was slow, sloppy, and easily dodged. I grabbed a knife and extracted the horn, the demon falling to his knees with a howl.

Prize in hand, I flooded him with my magic, zapping it through his veins to his kill spot. While killing demons was sometimes necessary, whenever it happened, the bars on my goblin's cage got a little bit flimsier. But I couldn't let the asper walk away–they were notoriously vindictive, and even the threat of Malik would lose its potency after a while.

He winked into oblivion with a pop, right as a needle-like pain spiked through my left thigh. My leg buckled under me, my protective suit torn and the tip of his rattle embedded into my flesh. It hung there quivering even though he was dead and gone.

Ice-cold venom flooded my system. Shaking violently, I fumbled at the stinger with fingers growing stiff and numb, but when I tore it free, my fuzzy brain was unable to process what I was supposed to do next.

A sudden spasm wracked my frame and stole the breath from my lungs. I crashed sideways against the wall, smashing my head against the concrete. The sharp bite of pain kicked me into clarity. *Get the venom out.*

Extracting poison was essentially the same process as extracting blood. I sent my magic into the affected area and drew the poison out in black pinpricks that welled up through my skin. The second it was all removed into a sticky resin ball that I easily and safely disposed of, I collapsed in a soggy heap on the floor, the sweat on my body drying into a clammy chill, as I used the last of my healing magic to seal the wound.

"We don't get paid extra for killing them. What if he was going to hire us to get his loot back from the daeva? You could've cost us a client." Harry prodded me with his scuffed loafer, his unlit cigarette clenched in his grip.

"Oh, please. Only one of us was getting out of the room and you know it. Figured you'd rather have had it be me," I mumbled, hugging myself for warmth.

"Tough call. I don't have to pay him benefits."

"What benefits?" I said through chattering teeth. "You pay slightly better than Ebenezer Scrooge and *his* employees got Christmas off."

"Heh. But you're rich in life experience." He left the room, returning momentarily with a thin cotton blanket, which he draped over me. "Get up."

The shock suffered from demon encounters was an often-enough occurrence in our office that Harry kept one of those warming closets for blankets on hand, like in a hospital.

I pulled the blanket up to my chin, grateful for the soothing heat. "Laying here and dying."

He wrenched me to my feet. For a bony old guy, he was very strong. "You are not dying. Do you understand?"

I shook his hands off from their death grip on my shoulders, retrieved the blanket that had slipped off, and wrapped it around myself. Much better. "You're not still upset about my final battle shenanigans—"

"Shenanigans?" Harry crushed his cigarette so hard the tobacco spilled out both ends. "Oh, wait. Are you perhaps referring to that one time you nearly killed yourself on national television?"

I winced. Yup, still upset.

A month ago, I'd tried to let a demon who ate magic take mine. Nee—my nickname for my bestie Nava—had needed bait and I had hoped becoming magicless would be my ticket to a normal life. That I could finally be a regular human, not a snack-addict half-redcap who had a thing for blood. When I'd seen the chance to rid myself of my powers during the battle, I'd jumped on the opportunity. I'd scared the pants off several people, an infuriating Italian one in particular, and given Harry a slight heart attack as he watched via livestream.

"I didn't know that losing my magic would also mean losing my life!" I stomped my foot. "Can we move past this already? I swear it's not suicide if I didn't intend to die."

Harry grunted and picked up the daeva horn between his thumb and forefinger. "I want out, Leo. I'm old, I'm tired, and I want to sit on a beach and paint goddamn watercolors. I've had enough excitement for ten lifetimes."

"I know." I took the horn from him and cleaned it off with the edge of the blanket.

"Then prove to me that in a couple of years, when you're finished your degree and you have your P.I. license, you'll be ready to take over."

Pride swelled in my chest. "Your business won't fail in my hands."

He wanted closure on this chapter of his life and I was key to that. I could relate. I wished that I'd had closure with the spawn that had sired me, and that my mother could get over that "guy" who'd gotten her pregnant. It was tough to move forward when one foot was stuck in the tar pit of the past. When one part of your life remained unresolved.

"That's not what I'm talking about," he said. "You have a harder road than most, kiddo. Not denying it. But if you're really serious about this as a lifestyle, you gotta make peace with who you are."

"I have. I swear it. I truly didn't know the consequences, and now that I do, I'd never do that to you." I handed him the horn to put away for safe-keeping until the daeva came to claim it.

He shook his head at me with a long-suffering look and left.

I was the kid Harry had never had and he was the closest thing to a dad in my life. Kobold, the redcap goblin that had knocked Mom up, didn't count. Oh, he'd made an effort in his own terrorizing way when I was younger, stealing into my room in the dead of night to "educate" me about my rightful heritage. Usually in the form of fucked-up games to draw out my redcap side. That all ended about six years ago, shortly after my fifteenth birthday, when I'd declared I was Team Human and refused to play. Kobold had threatened to kill me, so I'd called his bluff, banking on the fact that I was his only progeny and he was obsessed with someone carrying on his line.

He'd blinked first in our game of chicken, but not before leaving me with a three-inch scar across my abdomen. Something to remember him by. His last words were that my nature would win out and when it did, he'd be here to witness it.

We didn't exchange Christmas cards.

I flexed my fingers. The feeling had returned to my extremities, so I peeled off the wrecked protective suit, glad to be back in my slightly sweaty silver velvet leggings and a rust-colored velvet tunic. I put on my silver jewelry: rings, jangling bracelets, and small hoops in my ears to match my eyebrow ring, feeling more like myself.

Some women took on the world with a great lipstick or a pair of kickass heels. For me, it was these dozen shiny accessories that armored me up and let me move through life wrapped in my own pretty treasure trove.

The music snapped off. Mahler was bad enough. No music was code red.

I dumped the blanket in the hamper next to the warming closet that was also kept in the kitchen and went into the front office.

Harry sat there, holding but not drinking his customary mug of tea. His computer looked so forlorn without the jumble of UFO toys. Most of the models had been kept at home, but he'd had a bunch of them on top of his old clunky monitor, along with some alien figurines I'd found for him over the years.

He'd trashed them all on his sixty-fifth birthday in a bout of drunken disillusionment, and taken up watercolors. His technique was solid enough, but whenever he painted people or animals, there was always something uncannily off and vaguely disturbing. I held out hope he'd improve because I really didn't want any more eerie kitten canvases around the office. Their eyes followed me and not in a fun "Scooby Doo" way.

I turned a painting of an especially spooky Siamese cat on Harry's desk backwards so it wouldn't glower at me. "I'm not gonna hurt myself."

"Stop doing that." He grumpily returned the picture back to normal. "I'm proud of this one."

"May I please have my phone now?"

"Your generation needs to get off social media. It's toxic. Go see a friend instead." He slid it under a stack of folders.

I snatched it away and immediately opened a browser window. It was the same news we'd had since demons became public knowledge. A lot of proselytizing about humanity's fate and updates on government treaties with witches and Rasha. There was also speculation about whether the Israeli government would be allowed to try Rabbi Mandelbaum for attempting to unleash the apocalypse in Jerusalem or whether this was something for the International Court of Justice.

A headline screamed out at me: *Witches and Rasha! They're the new celeb couples, but will this sexy and magical engagement last?*

Underneath was a photo of a tall, willowy, Italian beauty, all dark hair and doe eyes, sporting quite the rock on her finger. And holding her hand?

Drio Rossi. The man who, despite having terrible pitch and impressively bad range, had sung his heart out to me just over a week ago and then showered me in Italian endearments. He'd had a rule about not kissing anyone since the love of his life had been murdered, but he'd broken it, all for me. And despite his nonstop sarcasm and an arrogance that was so massive, I swear it had a moon and gravitational pull, he'd honestly been kind of perfect—until he'd hied off across the ocean and maintained radio silence where I was concerned.

The picture of the happy couple shook in my hand. Guess I knew why he hadn't called.

2

I'd never been engulfed by a swarm of wasps, but I suspected it was very similar to what I felt at that moment. Goosebumps danced over hot and flushed patches of skin, and a loud buzzing filled my ears. I held myself absolutely still, not even blinking.

Harry opened his mouth to say something, then saw the look on my face and shut it at warp speed.

I grabbed my battered leather jacket and helmet off the row of hooks at the office front door and headed out to my silver-blue Vespa.

Harry watched me through the front glass window the entire time.

Tucking my hair under the helmet, I snagged the keys from my jacket pocket, settled myself on the bike, and turned the key. Once the dashboard lit up, I pulled one of the brake handles, and punched the start button. The Vespa, my precious baby, purred to life.

Vancouver in early October was my favorite time of year. The trees dotting the median on the main street beyond our strip mall parking lot blazed in brilliant reds and gold, and the sidewalk was a sea of crunchy color. The air had that bite to it that made me want to curl up in front of a wood fireplace, snug under one of my hand-knit blankets.

Right now, I failed to give a damn about any of it.

Conscious of Harry's gaze on me, I rode nice and slow out onto the street. Then I opened the Vespa up and tore through the world in a blur, welcoming the wind's sting.

My entire life was a struggle to live in the light. To get up every single day and re-commit myself to my humanity. It was so hard to keep from being consumed by my darkness.

A few years ago, one of Nava's cousins had married a non-Jewish woman who'd converted. While all of Nee's family was pretty secular, this woman became Jewish with a vengeance. Some of her family joked about it, but to me this over-compensation made sense. She wanted to belong to something that was important to her, but wasn't her birthright. It wasn't exactly the same for me, sure. I was partly human, for starters. But I also had to hold myself to a higher standard to compensate for the half that wasn't.

Maybe it was hypocritical of me, the big advocate for seeing the world in shades of gray, to be so black-and-white when it came to myself, but the severity got me through each day. And believe me, I was so damn grateful and happy for every moment I was human. But despite those tiny triumphs, living between two worlds was lonely.

Meeting Drio had been like finding a lighthouse. He harbored so much darkness, so many shadows, and yet the more I got to know him, the more I saw him constantly choosing the light in his own way. His demons may have lurked right behind his eyes, but they never clawed their way to the surface like I was scared mine would.

As we grew closer, he'd turned this blinding attention and affection on me that was only slightly less powerful in wattage than the sun. It wasn't about sex or romantic love. It was finding another person who could soothe your beast and reflected back your brilliance. Being with him had eased something deep in my soul.

When it came out that I was a half-demon, it was like a total solar eclipse. Drio threatened to kill me. All that light was not only snuffed out, the darkness that replaced it was suffocating, a jagged hatred that cut deeper than any wound. I didn't need the "love of a good man" or some such bullshit to save or validate me, but I saw a lifetime of loneliness yawning out ahead of me like a giant crevasse and it made me want to weep.

I thought Drio had truly seen me. Recognized me for what I was, because in many ways it was what he was as well.

I thought wrong.

And I'd accepted it, moved on, and decided I would deal with a long, lonely life, except then came my friend Rohan Mitra's concert in Los Angeles. That was the night Drio had pulled this stupid stunt and sung Frankie Valli's "Can't Take My Eyes Off of You" to me. A single, fragile hope had bloomed in my chest, but I'd ruthlessly refused to let it take root too deeply. I'd allowed Drio to drive me back to the hotel I was staying at, but I hadn't let him come up.

I didn't want a relationship based on grand gestures or wildly fluctuating ups and downs. Wearing a pretty outfit and standing under glittering lights and the seductive cover of night made it easy to believe in a future together. We needed to make it in the cold, hard light of day.

I'd told him that when he came back, we could take things slow and smart and build something real. Except slow, smart, and real never happened.

He'd gone to Italy to convince the scary head of the Italian coven to give her blessing for a witch-Rasha training facility in Rome so both communities could establish a new demon hunting base there. He didn't call; I didn't call.

Even if I did hope.

I knew better now. There'd be no Cinderella story, no

happily-ever-after. Just Drio, gone again, while I picked up the pieces and vowed to purge him from my system once and for all.

I pulled into the parking space behind my apartment building in the West End. Entering the lobby, I greeted the two women around my age who had recently moved in. This old building only had sixteen units, so there was no anonymity. Knowing my neighbors and feeling like part of a community was worth the faded lobby carpet that smelled vaguely of cat and the elevator that mysteriously stopped working for most of the winter.

My open-concept apartment was silent and still when I let myself in. A bright Andy Warhol print of flowers dominated the wall above my sofa, next to the comfy chair and coffee table grouped on the fluffy area rug in front of my TV. Beyond that was a small dining area and a narrow galley kitchen. Three doors led off the living room. One led to my bedroom, one to my bathroom, and the third to my front door.

It was a cozy place and I often entertained, but I'd never shared it permanently with anyone. Much like my life. Way easier to hold most people at arm's length, especially when I continued to suffer the odd nightmare that I'd gone full-goblin, murdering hapless humans and fashioning a cap as we did to dip in our victim's blood, while Kobold laughed, only to wake in the dead of night, gasping.

I curled onto my couch, dragging my latest knit blanket over my legs. I usually made soft throws in rainbow colors but this one was deep black.

A minute later, my best friend Nava appeared in front of me, having portalled directly into my apartment. I barely startled, now very used to her comings and goings. She may have saved the world, but she hadn't mastered the art of phoning ahead.

Her curly dark brown hair was pulled into a high ponytail and she wore a cute yellow plaid mini skirt with a tight black sweater. She held up the two pizza boxes in her hands, oozing with the smell of cheese and pork products. "It's been a while since we've pigged out and vegged."

"Nice try, Nee. You saw the article."

She blinked innocently. "What article?"

"You're a terrible liar. Is Snowflake busy tonight?"

"No." She shoved one of the boxes at me. "For implying I'm some kind of clingy chick who can only see her friends when her boyfriend isn't available, you get the Hawaiian pizza."

I slapped the box away. It flipped onto my leather sofa, the lid still closed. "Pineapple on pizza is an abomination."

She shrugged and sank on to the couch. "Pick it off."

"Gimme the meat lover's."

Nava grabbed her crotch. "Take it."

I grimaced. "Phrasing!"

She scrunched up her face. "That verbal-action combo didn't come out right."

"I mean, am I supposed to go for your personal meat lover or the pizza?"

"I think it was open to interpretation and your own read of the situation," she said.

Taking the meat lover's pizza away from her, I dumped it on the coffee table, next to the two cans of chilled Coke that she had brought along with a roll of paper towels, because we were classy that way.

"Grab my wallet," I said. "I'll pay half."

"Nah, my treat. You don't have to subsidize me yet."

Nava's salary as a demon hunter had been paid by the Brotherhood of David. Once she and her allies had taken down the corrupt rabbi leader of that organization, all its hefty bank accounts, corporate assets, and real estate holdings had been frozen. A team of lawyers was working to determine ownership and transfer all this capital to the new witch-Rasha council. As it had been less than a month since all this had gone down, all demon hunting was happening on a pro bono/good karma basis.

Additionally, Nava was busy setting up a program to mentor

at-risk witches. She was the happiest I'd seen her in years, and if it weren't for pesky things like rent and food, she wouldn't have cared about being paid at all.

Personally, I voted for mooching off her rock star boyfriend, but she refused. Not that Rohan would mind. He wasn't a materialistic guy, but he'd gift her the world just to make her smile. It was in every look he bestowed on her.

Once, Drio had looked at me that way. I fiddled with the edge of the blanket.

"Nice color," Nava said. "Is it Drio's Soul Black? You know, there's no way he's engaged. He *sang* to you."

"We all do things at night that we regret in the light of day. Drio's done yet another about-face where I'm concerned. This should come as a surprise to no one." Given how many times he'd threatened to kill me for being a half-demon, it was silly to believe that he'd genuinely reconciled his past with any future we might have together.

More fool I.

"That's it?" Nava snagged a piece of pizza.

"For now," I said.

"And later?"

"I'm going to Rome to force him to man up and end this face-to-face. Then I'll stab him." Nope. No qualms with violence in his case. I grabbed my first slice of salami, prosciutto, and pancetta pizza. It was so hot that I juggled it between my hands, blowing on the cheese. "Then I'll have surface-breaking sex with someone. I might do that part both before and after the stabbing. Haven't decided."

"Good plan," she said. "But properly talk to him before you kill him?"

"Oh, I'm not killing him. I want excruciating, drawn-out pain that will be his only company through the rest of his long, lonely, miserable life."

Nava pushed the Coke can away from me. "Maybe hold off on the caffeine."

Patience was not my strong suit where food was concerned, and I ate half of the piece in one go, despite the mozzarella being still hot enough to burn the roof of my mouth. While I ate, I studied the engagement photo on my phone like I could X-ray vision my way to an explanation. They looked so happy together, her arm tucked under his like they'd known each other their whole lives.

First rule of being a P.I: appearances are deceiving.

"I really want to stab him and be done with it," I said, "but this doesn't make sense. Grr. Why can't I just hate him instead of needing answers?"

I blamed math. When I was younger, that had been my favorite subject because every equation was resolvable. There was something so clean and satisfying about solving for X. In my current line of work, "X" was infinitely more complex but that just made it more fascinating. I loved being faced with a puzzle to crack, not just thinking methodically, but having to also think on my feet to rule out all the variables at play until I had a single irrefutable answer. The more baffling the mystery, the more invested I got.

Nava wiped her hands on a piece of paper towel. "Because you aren't a drama queen and this matters."

"Could he be on an undercover mission?" I said. "Does Ro know anything?"

She shook her head. "No, he's baffled, but he doesn't believe it's true. I dunno about an undercover job. However, apparently Antonia D'Amico, the old witch he was sent to woo, is a total strega nonna and her hatred of Rasha knows no bounds. I bet she's torturing him."

"A girl can dream, but engagement to a beautiful woman is hardly torture."

"Maybe his fiancée is a demon," she said.

"That would torture him if he'd been forced in some way, but why do it? Also, where'd you get your information about Antonia?"

Nava's tongue darted out to catch an errant pineapple nugget. "I am now an important figure within the witch community and people wish to tell me things."

"You paid someone?" A thin string of mozza stretched from my mouth to my slice. I cut through it with my finger, sucking it back, before chowing down on my second piece. Being brutally injured required a lot of food to refill the tank, and what delicious fuel this was.

"Not so much paying as extreme communal bartering. I got Rivka to hand over Esther's rugelach recipe, which I traded to Sienna for information and two dozen rugelach to be shared with Rivka, provided Sienna doesn't botch the cinnamon."

"Wow, that does sound extreme."

Nava nudged my leg. "Hostage negotiations require less delicacy, but you're worth it."

I blew her a kiss. "I need Ada and my friendly neighborhood hacker."

Named after Ada Lovelace, Lord Byron's daughter and a pioneer of computing technology, Ada was an evolving database drawing on intelligence from the witch and Rasha communities. She'd also been designed to integrate access to the demon dark web. I was only taking two classes at Simon Fraser University this semester, Intro to Cybercrime and a directed readings course, so my load was fairly light. If Harry didn't need me, I spent my time off with my friend Kane Hashimoto and Pierre, another Rasha, working on Ada.

We stashed the rest of the pizza in the fridge and then Nava portalled us to her twin brother Ari and his boyfriend Kane's apartment, not far from mine.

Ari sauntered into the spare bedroom that had been converted into an office. Blond and badass in all-black clothing that clung to his muscled frame, there was zero trace of the geeky kid I'd befriended at thirteen. He placed a cup of coffee on Kane's desk. "Do you ever use the front door?"

Nava shot him a look like he was an idiot for even asking.

Harry's office may have been sweetly ramshackle, but Kane's work space made it look like a desperate hovel in comparison. For a man with the most horrific taste in clothing, like today's shirt covered in random blobs of color that he'd paired with silver pants, his design sense was flawless. Streamlined adjustable desks in dark espresso were paired with modern ergonomic white and chrome chairs. Jade plants graced the windowsill and surrealist prints by Ari's favorite painters hung on the cream walls. Kane had blushed adorably when I'd teased him about that.

"Just mainline the caffeine in, darling boy." Kane's spiky black hair was crazier than normal, which meant he'd been working out a coding problem and running his fingers through it. He rolled out his shoulder, the pecs on his sculpted torso clenching under his skintight shirt.

Ari was immediately at his side, massaging his shoulder. Kane tipped his head back, beaming up at his boyfriend with a brilliant smile.

Kane had been the one who ended up playing bait and giving up his magic during that end-of-the-world showdown, and I'd never seen him happier. He remained key to the on-going fight against evil through his work with Ada, but he'd had his fill of hunting, and now was able to live his life with the man of his dreams.

Ari was thriving as well. He'd taken over as head of training for all Rasha and witches, now that Baruch Ya'ari, the former Rasha in the position, was busy appeasing the world's governments.

"I need your help," I said.

Kane wheeled his chair over to me and tapped my thigh. "Hell no, he is not engaged. I saw him at Ro-Ro's concert. Drio was besotted with you."

"Besotted?" Ari said. He threw hands up at Kane's glower.

"I'm voting for lobotomy or clone." I sat down at the desk

I'd been given when I came to work with Kane and logged in to Ada. "But we can't rule anything out."

My friends all chimed in with their theories, but I told everyone to hold their opinions for the time being. Given the depraved clients we dealt with, Harry had trained me to set all judgments aside until the facts were in. P.I. rule number two.

"We'll go through everything with a fine-toothed comb," Nava said. She'd do her best to help me, they all would, and my friends were smart and savvy, but even the most experienced of us missed the occasional detail.

Like, had Nava looked closely at the blanket that I'd knit, she'd have seen that it wasn't all black. In one corner was a tiny brilliant silver star. See, Nava had been wrong–the blanket wasn't Drio. It was me. I'd shone through darkness before and I would shine through this.

But it wasn't the dark that got you; it was the monsters hiding there, and before this was over, I'd come face-to-face with the scariest one of all.

3

Nava peered over my shoulder. "Find anything?"

"Not about this." I fired off a quick email to our Rasha friend Mahmud about a possible demon attack in Baghdad since he now coordinated where everyone was deployed to hunt.

Kane, Ari, and Nava had amassed the life story of the strega nonna, the grandmother witch that Drio had been sent to convince to set up the training facility.

"Antonia is seventy-five years old and she's held the title of coven head for all of Italy for fifty years," Nava said.

"Yikes," I said.

"Bet she eliminated the competition but good. She's Sicilian." Kane cracked his knuckles. "They're sleeping with the fishes."

"Still doesn't explain how Drio ended up engaged to her granddaughter," Ari said.

I read the spooling pages coming off the printer. "Well, Drio *has* been punched in the head a lot. Maybe he got confused as to which female in that family he was supposed to win over."

"Or Antonia enchanted him to fall in love with her granddaughter," Nava said.

"Would you?" I said. "I mean yeah, he's a pretty face, but unless Antonia hates the poor girl, she'd want a real contender. Dubiously civilized, deeply dark, and barely healed men generally are not considered catches."

"Pfft. You considered it pretty hard for a while there," Kane pointed out.

"Well, d'uh. That combo is my catnip. But I'm a half-demon." I pointed at the fiancée in the engagement photo attached to the gossip article. "This woman looks like a fairy princess. She even has a princess name. Isabella Aria De Luca." I sifted through the papers. "Antonia is on record as being virulently anti-Rasha. So why send Drio to change her mind? Why not another witch? Unless she'd met him before?" I grabbed a pen. "Everything we know about Drio. Go."

We ended up calling in the big guns: Rohan. Drio's best friend.

With the dusting of stubble against his dark brown skin, his hair that had grown slightly too long curling wildly around his ears, and his gold eyes sparkling against the green cashmere sweater and black tailored pants he wore, Rohan was one of the hottest guys I'd ever seen. I'd been madly in love with him in my teens when he'd fronted the supergroup Fugue State Five. Now, I objectively could appreciate his handsomeness, but he didn't make my pulse flutter or my insides clench. Sisterhood code with Nava and all that.

Ari ushered us all into the living room where he'd already set out food and drinks. Nava had trained him well in the snack supply department.

Rohan squeezed my shoulder, but he kept any pity to himself and let me quiz him about Drio's life. I wrote his answers on a chart pinned to the living room wall.

Kane was particular about a lot of things, like the modern furniture he was carefully amassing piece-by-piece, or the bright artwork by local Vancouver painters on the robin's egg blue walls. I'd expected him to kick up a fuss about the thumbtacks holding the chart, but he said that crime investigations took precedence.

What Rohan couldn't remember about Drio, such as the elementary school he'd gone to, or how old Drio's parents were when he was born, Kane tracked down, his fingers flying over his keyboard clacking out a rapid rhythm.

Nava, meantime, called our friend Raquel to learn more about this assignment.

"Raquel said Drio contacted her and volunteered." Nava tossed her phone on the side table with the artfully arranged cacti next to the suede couch. It dinged off one of the planters.

Kane immediately straightened it so the plants were once more precisely lined up.

Ari rolled his eyes and Nava grinned.

"You chose him," she said.

Kane humphed and plugged his laptop in.

I dropped into a brown leather club chair with my feet tucked under my butt. A tendril of doubt snaked through me. He'd volunteered? Well, he lived in Rome. Maybe he and Isabella had known each other for a while. Maybe I was the element that didn't make sense, not her. Maybe the engagement was real. "Did Raquel say why?"

"No," Nava said. "He'd heard about Antonia blocking the new training facility and he offered to help. To be fair, Raquel is so busy meeting with different factions right now to establish legal protections for witches that I doubt she probed too deeply. This was one thing off her plate and she took the help where she could." She settled into the crook of Rohan's arm.

Ro had been busy since his performance doing press for his album, setting up tour dates, and still keeping to a hunting schedule. He should have been exhausted, but leaning against his girlfriend, he was the picture of contented bliss.

I spun the pen between my fingers, examining the chart. "We've got Drio's, Antonia's, and Isabella's life stories in bullet points. What we don't have is any intersection between him and the women. Again, why volunteer?"

"Drio has a soft spot for old women," Ro said.

We all stared at him.

"Not like that, you sickos."

Nava snapped her fingers. "That's right. Golda."

"Golda is the widow of the rabbi who was head of the L.A. chapter while we were initiates there," Rohan said. "Even after Drio moved back to Rome, they stayed close. He still visits her. There's got to be a personal connection with Antonia, because with Drio it's either you're in his inner circle or you're dead to him. And if he doesn't know you, you're still dead to him until you prove your worth."

"No kidding." Nava dug into a bowl of buttery popcorn and scooped out a handful.

"Parents." Kane and Ari said in unison.

Nava fired a popcorn kernel at Kane, sitting on the love seat across from her and Rohan. "My twin. Only I mind meld with him."

Grimacing, Kane dug the kernel out of the sofa cushions. "Those days are over, babyslay."

Nava and Ari exchanged a bittersweet look.

"I guess they are," she said.

Kane threw the kernel back at her. "Please. You two spent the entire night last week at your parents' dinner finishing each other sentences. I almost brained the both of you."

She perked up and Ari shot Kane a grateful smile.

"Very sweet. Back to parents. What did you guys mean?" I ate a handful of salt and vinegar chips.

"Isabella and Drio have parents around the same age," Ari said. "They could be the connection."

Rohan checked his phone. "It's too late to phone Drio's parents in Italy."

Kane was already typing. "Don't need them."

Nava and Ari debated takeout options while we waited for

the tech genius to pony up his results. She held up two menus. "Ari and Kane want sushi. Leo and I want Chinese."

"You just had pizza," I said.

"A snack, hours ago. I could eat again. You could eat again."

I snorted at the massive understatement. Her metabolism was almost as fast as mine, and mine was demonically-induced.

"Perhaps you should ask Leo what she wants," Kane groused, "instead of casting her vote with you because you want to win."

"I want Thai," I said.

"See?" Kane gloated.

"No." Nava waved the flyer for Chinese food at me with an exasperated hand flap. "You want spicy squid and gai lan."

My mouth watered. "Oh, yeah. I do want that. And a double order of onion pancakes."

"Obviously," she said. "Rohan, decide."

He cocked an eyebrow. "Really decide or Nava decide?"

"Really decide. I'm not a monster."

He glanced at Ari, who shook his head. "Nee says that, and then you find a snake in your bed because she didn't get her hot and sour soup."

Rohan considered it for a moment, then said, "Chinese."

"Really?" Nava said.

"Sparky," he warned.

She danced over to him and kissed his cheek. "You never had a choice."

"I'm well aware," he said, training a fond smile on her.

She held out her hand. "Help me order."

Ro happily followed her into the kitchen.

"Remember, Kane and I eat in there," Ari called out. "Don't gross up any surfaces."

I crammed some chips into my mouth without tasting them, weighing whether my favorite Chinese food was worth being around two nauseatingly happy couples any longer.

Kane looked up from his laptop. "Their moms were room-mates at boarding school."

"Drio's mother is American," I said around a mouthful of chips. "Is Isabella's?"

"No, she's Italian, but she went to school in the States. They don't seem to have kept in touch as adults beyond Facebook friends, but we have the connection."

Drio was close to his parents and it was plausible that he'd gone to see Antonia at his mother's request. What had happened between him leaving Los Angeles on September 28 and me finding out about his engagement today, eleven days later?

Rohan wandered over to the chart, then beckoned me across the room.

"He hasn't contacted any of us," Rohan said. "You don't think that's odd?"

I patted his cheek. "I don't have the best barometer of what's normal behavior for him, but it's adorable that you besties touch base regularly."

Something on the chart caught his attention. "Isabella is doing her Master's degree in Early Childhood Education and volunteers at an animal shelter?"

I ground my teeth. Wow, he had really gone for a woman who darkness never touched. "She's pretty awesome."

He chuckled. "Leo, do you know what Asha was studying?"

I shook my head, unsure why this mattered when Drio was literally about to marry a living saint.

"Forensic science, specializing in bloodstain pattern analysis."

"Like *Dexter*? Cool!" My goblin half loved blood, but this fascinated my human side as well. Spatters were their own important part of puzzle solving, and I loved that scientists could recreate crimes from their trajectory.

"Right?" His face lit up. It was nice to see him able to think about his cousin—Drio's girlfriend who'd been murdered by a demon—without shadows chasing his expression. "Believe me when I say there is no fucking way he's willingly engaged to

Isabella. We've ruled out undercover work thanks to Mahmud, which leaves what, in your opinion?"

"Force. Either good old blackmail or magic compulsion. You'd have to get close to determine which one." Whatever had happened, Drio hadn't simply tossed me over. I took the first full breath that I had in hours.

"I'd like to hire you to find out definitively," Rohan said. "He may need help and he's stubborn enough to not ask for it."

"What? No. I have school and work and I can't afford to jaunt off to Italy. You go."

Rohan shook his head, his expression grave. "Nava and I are too well-known. Our involvement could make the situation worse, and I don't trust anyone else with his well-being. You're trained to deal with magic, you're a good investigator, and you can handle yourself. Find out what's happened to Drio. For me. I'll square it with Harry," Rohan said. "Make it an official case and cover your travel expenses."

I bit my lip. On the one hand, Drio and a possible homicide charge. On the other, Italy. And a possible homicide charge.

Rohan got a mischievous gleam in his eyes. "Come on. Once Drio is safe, you can make him suffer."

"Nice best friend there, Ro."

He shrugged, looking completely unrepentant. "He threatened to kill you on more than one occasion. *He crashed my gig.*"

I laughed. "Yes. Upstaging you at your performance was the more heinous crime."

Ro furrowed his brow. "Who said anything about upstaging? He sang like a stuck pig and my name is attached to that."

"Poor baby. Upset that his song has gotten more views than your performance?"

"How would you know that?" He smirked. "Psychic ability? Divine intuition? Watching them both multiple times?"

"You are spending entirely too much time with that girl-friend of yours."

"Probably. Will you take the case?"

No job left unresolved. If I took it, I'd be promising to see this through to the end, no matter how hard it got. Even if Drio was being forced to play along, I'd still have to watch him be with another woman. But Drio was absolutely stubborn enough to try and get out of a sticky situation without help.

"Fine," I said. "But the stabbing is still on the table. A girl has to have a Plan B."

4

Nava showed up at my apartment at 5AM on Thursday morning. She stuffed her gloves into the pockets of her green plaid duffel coat and yawned, making it sound accusing. "Friends don't make friends get up at this hour."

"If I didn't have to account for a nine-hour time difference, I wouldn't be awake either." I adjusted the strap of my bulging messenger bag which contained a couple changes of clothing and a few items that might come in handy. I'd shown remarkable self-control and left out my Taser. "Love the elbow patches."

"I really think 2010 was an underrated year, fashion-wise, and I'm helping it make a comeback." Nava had lost most of her clothing in a fire that had consumed the Vancouver chapter of the Brotherhood where she'd lived. Without a paycheck, she'd been reduced to foraging through old clothes left behind at her parents' house when she'd moved out. "You're looking very high-end today," she said.

That was because I had a role to play. I'd foregone my beloved velvet clothing and silver jewelry, and the psychological protection they afforded me, for tailored black slacks that were deceptively stretchy and a fitted moss green sweater. I completed the look with high-heeled black pumps. My red hair was pulled into a high ponytail with a thick ribbon wrapped around it.

"People are more inclined to let you in to a building if you don't look like you intend to rob the place. My regular vibe is too bohemian." I shrugged into a black wool trench coat that I'd picked up on a cross-border shopping trip to Nordstrom Rack in Washington State and braced myself.

Nava portalled us to Rome, depositing us in a narrow, cobblestone lane several blocks away from Drio's building which was located in the Trastevere neighborhood on the west bank of the Tiber River. We startled a tiny white Maltese puppy peeking out of a backpack. It started yapping but its owner was so engrossed in her phone conversation that she didn't do more than reach back and give it a half-hearted pat.

I yawned, having to always pop my ear drums after I'd portalled. The upside about magic now out in the open? No worrying about inducing mass panic. Done and done.

We wandered over to the end of the block where it intersected a busier road. Drivers in tiny Fiats honked impatiently at gawking tourists, while locals in cafés argued loudly. The streets were filled with cigarette smoke and chatter. Everyone was gloriously vibrant and alive, from the stylish women to the boisterous men in tight shirts secure in their masculinity as they kissed each other on both cheeks.

Nee and I drank it in.

"Is it everything you hoped for?" she said.

"Better." Growing up, my mom had been a big Audrey Hepburn fan and we'd watched *Roman Holiday* a gazillion times together. I'd decided that when I grew up, I'd have a Vespa and move to Italy. Now that I was actually here, I was falling even harder under its spell. "New plan. Kill Drio and take his apartment."

"Only if it has a guest room. Ro and I need somewhere to stay."

"You can stay in a hotel," I said. "I'm not subjecting myself to your monkey sex."

"Ew. That makes it sound like we fling poo at each other."

We snickered at the mental image, having the combined emotional age of a six-year-old at times, and crossed the road, weaving through traffic that had momentarily come to a standstill as a van maneuvered into an impossibly narrow garage door.

The route to Drio's building took us through a spacious piazza, anchored at one end by a large stone fountain. Backpackers hung out on the stairs ringing the base and the smell of baked dough hung in the air.

"You should probably eat before you confront him," Nava said.

"And you need an espresso for the road."

We ducked into a tiny café and stood at the marble bar. The barista, a woman with her hair pulled into a glossy bun and rocking red lipstick, took our order.

"Due caffè con panna per favore." I perused the few food offerings in the glass case and pointed at the cookies. "E due biscotti."

I'd spent many hours during stakeouts listening to Italian-language podcasts and was now moderately fluent in tourist-level Italian and swearing. Thanks to years of French Immersion, the language wasn't very hard for me to pick up.

The barista set our biscotti out on plates and then worked the gleaming copper espresso-maker like a pro, quickly presenting us with two tiny white cups on saucers. Steam curled off the black espresso, a perfect dollop of whipped cream floating in the center of each like a miniature cloud.

I inhaled the rich, bitter brew.

We stood at the bar since sitting down at the little round tables automatically jacked up the bill, and honestly, we'd be done in a couple of minutes.

Nava dipped her biscotti in the espresso. "If I didn't have to get back to work, I'd tell you to blow off the assignment and we could spend all day eating."

"We'll do that eventually." I paid with some euro I'd gotten before leaving, making sure to get a receipt. This was an official job after all, so Ro was on the hook for my expenses.

"Should I pay for myself?" Nava frowned.

"Nope. You're line item 'transportation.' You get fed on the client's dime." We stepped outside.

"Had I known this was on the expense account I'd have had a second biscotti. Call me when you want to come home."

"Will do. Schmugs." Our secret best friend signoff.

"Schmugs." Nava threw me a finger wave over her shoulder as she headed around the corner and was lost to view.

Antonia lived outside Florence in a tiny village, but Drio and Isabella had decamped to Rome. I'd sifted through all the online photos I could find of them—and there were a lot—to narrow down their location.

The masses that weren't repulsed by the idea of witches and Rasha were obsessed with them. Sales of Rohan's new album had skyrocketed, and I'm sure this engagement was pulling in the online views. It didn't hurt that Drio and Isabella were insane eye candy. I'd totally have gone for her and how fucked up was that?

Paparazzi had been hanging around this one particular apartment building to catch their comings and goings. It was about four stories high, painted a pale butterscotch with charming shuttered windows and stone work along the bottom of the medieval architecture. The arched wood front door studded with iron bolts had a giant knocker in the shape of a lion's head.

It was the kind of building I'd dreamed of living in.

Figured Drio lived here.

There was a small fruit market at the corner of his block, and I browsed the merchandise, watching the front door, but concluded there was too much foot traffic to pick the lock.

I sauntered closer and examined the list of names next to the entry phone. Drio wasn't on there, but as a Rasha, I wouldn't expect him to list his name. It didn't matter, Kane had gotten his address for me. He was on the third floor in the front right apartment.

While there weren't any obvious security cameras trained on the door, I didn't want to rule that possibility out.

I rang Drio's apartment a few times, but no one answered. Not an absolute guarantee that he and Isabella were out, though the possibility was likely. Most of the other occupants I rang weren't home either, which wasn't surprising since it was the middle of the afternoon. The time of day worked in my favor and was the reason I'd timed my visit as I had. Less people around to ask questions once I got inside.

I got lucky on my fifth attempt and a man with a bad cold answered the intercom. I jabbered at him in rapid, distressed French. Speak English in Europe without a British accent and the locals would immediately peg you as American, which, fair or not, made them disinclined to help. I'd learned that the hard way on a job in Barcelona last year. At least with my French, they assumed I was from the continent.

The man grunted something and buzzed me in.

The wood door was so thick that it was a bit warped and I had to throw my shoulder against it to open it. It led to a small foyer that smelled like lavender, with large cream tiles and a gorgeous, well-oiled staircase curving up to the second floor. I ran my hand over the gleaming bannister, flicking a glance at the tiny cage elevator and immediately dismissing it. I wasn't getting in some rickety deathtrap. I took the stairs at a leisurely pace, alert to any doors opening or voices.

All was quiet.

When I got to the third floor, I knocked on Drio's door, but there was still no answer. I crouched down to examine his lock. Fucker. He had the Abloy Protec2 Deadbolt, a disk detainer lock that was impossible to pick. Even if I had a drill on me, the face of the deadbolt was made of a hardened steel that would chew up a dozen of the most expensive drill bits and still not allow access.

There were six other apartments on this floor, all of which featured standard deadbolts that I could pick in my sleep. I slipped my heels off, cramming them into my messenger bag, then I placed the bag and my rolled-up trench coat deep into a large, decorative vase with a fake tree that stood in a corner of the landing.

According to the photos that I'd sourced late last night, Drio had a single window on the side of the building, probably his bathroom. That would be my access point.

After verifying that his neighbor wasn't home, I pulled two bobby pins out of my hair and made quick work of their lock. I slipped inside, closing the neighbor's apartment door silently behind me, and taking a moment in the small entryway to listen for any dogs or parrots that might sound an alarm. It happened. Cats generally failed to give a damn.

I had slightly better hearing than most people, courtesy of my redcap side, and was able to quickly verify that the apartment was empty. Still, I tiptoed my way through the all-white apartment, testing the floorboards for squeaking. I wouldn't want to alert a downstairs neighbor to an intruder.

White walls, white furniture, white shag throw rugs, and a white statue of some jungle cat on the white-tiled fireplace, this home could have been lifted out of a Jackie Collins novel about Hollywood high living circa the 1980s. Books my mom was addicted to back when she still strived for dreams instead of bemoaning their loss. I missed that version of her.

A faint smell of tomato sauce permeated the air.

The bathroom continued with its monochromatic aesthetic, but give this owner their due—behind the toilet, the grout in the small shower, around the sink taps—everything was spotless. However, the window opened outward, which wasn't ideal. I would have preferred a sash window that opened straight up, but beggars couldn't be choosers.

Propping the window open, I leaned over the windowsill and glanced down, relieved to see there were no pigeon spikes on the narrow ledge that ran the length of the building. Boosting myself onto the counter, I carefully climbed out. There was a bit of a tricky moment keeping my balance while shutting the window, but I managed. It wasn't locked, but it had clicked shut so it would stay closed.

The building directly opposite me was empty, and none of the other windows I scanned showed any movement. The narrow, twisty street below me had a man pushing a small kiosk over the cobblestones and whistling, but was otherwise clear. I edged my way along the ledge until I came to the next window—Drio's.

It was locked from the inside with a latch. Nothing to pick.

Pulling the tall green shutters part-way closed to shield myself from prying eyes, I tugged the ribbon out of my hair. Sure, it matched my sweater, but it was also reinforced with a lightweight, flexible layer of metal. I wound the ribbon around my knuckles like a boxer's wrap and punched the glass next to the inside frame, careful not to hit too hard. A small section of the glass spiderwebbed. A couple more punches and I'd cracked it enough to push a piece of glass onto his bathroom floor. It was just wide enough to slip my hand through, which I managed without even nicking my skin, so big props to me. I unlatched the window, then hopped inside.

I waited a bit longer in his bathroom listening for any signs of life than I had in the neighbor's place. If Drio was under some spell or compulsion, I wasn't about to be surprised by a man with flash step magic. He'd probably react to my goblin side and attempt to kill me.

Again.

Murderously predictable Drio may have been, but his bathroom was utterly charming. Bastard. Small black diamond tiles accented the white squares on the floor. The toilet, pedestal sink, and clawfoot tub were also white and white tiles ran up the walls, broken only by a chair rail of narrow black tiles. A stunning black-and-white framed photograph of a naked woman's body, partially in shadow, was hung over the bathtub. The room was bright and airy, and I could easily imagine soaking in the tub, Drio sitting on the closed toilet lid, drinking coffee and talking about our day.

I rubbed the heel of my palm against my chest, but it didn't dispel the ache that settled there.

The rest of his apartment was suffused in warmth. A large Turkish rug in sumptuous orange, red, and blue blanketed the warm wooden planks in the living room, peppered with furniture that had been chosen for comfort.

More framed photography was hung on the walls, these pictures alive with color. There were gondoliers in their painted boats, a Bedouin in a deep blue headscarf leading a camel across the hot Sahara sand, and an Asian fisherman holding the day's catch on the shores of a turquoise sea.

The biggest surprise? A bookcase that took up an entire wall and was filled to overflowing with everything from pristine hardcovers to dog-eared paperbacks. There were a lot of psychology books from Drio's university days mixed in with non-fiction political works and thrillers by authors like Lee Child, Stieg Larsson, and Gillian Flynn both in English and translated into Italian. I smiled when I saw his collection of James Bond novels, remembering the night he'd confessed to going through a phase of introducing himself when he was about eleven as "Rossi. Drio Rossi."

Other than textbooks, everything I read was on my Kindle, but he clearly preferred the tangible experience of a physical book. My heart beat a little faster picturing him on the brown leather sofa with one of the pillows stuffed under his head, lost in a good story. An image that would likely only ever reside in my fantasy. I indulged it a moment, inhaling the light woodsy scent of his cologne, then shook my head, ordering myself to get my shit together.

Pulling a thin pair of gloves out of my bra, I methodically searched his apartment to eliminate the possibility that he was being controlled by a magic artifact. To do that, I had to hunt it out. If Drio and Isabella were being blackmailed or under a direct verbal compulsion either by a witch or a demon, I'd be shit-out-of-luck unless I found a clue that would point me to the agenda behind all this. However, if they were being compelled via artifacts, since there would need to be one for each of them, those items would complement each other in some way.

Despite searching every nook and cranny, there was nothing magical to be found. Other than the lube and dildo in the side drawer next to his bed that I tried very hard not to picture Drio using on himself. I clamped my legs together, squirming, and sat down on his king-sized mattress that dominated the bedroom.

Was it magic or was it blackmail? Either way, what purpose did this engagement serve? Antonia could have been lying about hating Rasha, and it was possible that even Isabella was the one compelling Drio, since she was a witch as well, but why? That's what I couldn't figure out.

Yet.

P.I. rule number three: be persistent enough and you're sure to find something.

A key turned in the lock outside.

I ran into the bathroom, hiding behind the door. If Drio was being blackmailed, I wouldn't be in any danger, other than from his hard-headedness at me showing up and trying to help. But if he was being compelled?

I had to see him and get a read on the situation. I glanced back at the window, assuring myself that a way out was close at hand, crept to the doorway, and froze. Isabella was with him. I'd expected it, but intellectually preparing myself did sweet fuck all against the reality of seeing him in his kitchen hanging out with my replacement.

My hands balled into fists. They were speaking Italian too quickly for me to get the gist, but neither of them sounded robotic or angry. Just super chill and normal, like how you'd expect talking to your loving fiancée would sound.

Isabella was dressed in dark jeans and a funky blazer with a filmy shirt underneath. She must have had a good eight inches to my five-foot-two, putting her much closer to Drio's six feet. A much easier kissable level.

My goblin woke up with a growl. Shit! Not now. I visualized amping up my inner white light, slowing the growth of her dark form.

Drio's blond hair was raked carelessly back from his face, his olive skin tanned deeper than the last time I'd seen him, causing his emerald green eyes to pop. He moved through the space with a lithe grace, touching the small of Isabella's back as he brushed past her. One of those carelessly intimate touches that lovers didn't even think about as he bestowed a tender smile on her.

That was the same smile I'd only ever received right before the first sweet kiss he'd given me. Correction, not even sweet. More a super chaste peck on the lips. What was he, five? He couldn't have kissed me properly that night?

Given the *besotted* answering look on Isabella's face, her eyes sparkling and two splotches of color on her cheeks, I bet he'd kissed *her* properly many times already.

My redcap scrabbled inside my brain, howling to eviscerate Isabella. I braced my palms against the wall, taking deep breaths.

Kudos to the mastermind behind all this: they'd certainly crossed all their T's and dotted their I's, because nothing about this looked compelled. They were either very good at what they did, or this engagement was real and I was severely deluded in my wishful thinking for a magic explanation.

I couldn't decide and every passing second landed me in greater danger. My body was shaking with the sheer force of will keeping my demon at bay. The world became awash in red. I flung myself towards the window and closed the toilet lid with sweaty hands, almost dropping it and giving myself away. That would be awesome. They'd come in here to investigate. I'd go for

Isabella's throat, Drio would go for mine, and Christmas would come early for the blood spatter analysts.

Climbing onto the toilet seat lid, I swung the window open, startling a window washer hanging there, working. There went my exit strategy.

I snarled at him, then dropped to the floor in a crouch, hidden from view by the tub, unsure of what to do. There was no way I could make it across the apartment to the front door without being seen.

My goblin didn't want to hide. She wanted to devour.

Teeth grinding together, I wrestled her into submission, my confusion and panic making this ten times harder. There were two reasons why she ever came out. I'd let myself get too hungry and run down, or the presence of blood. Neither was the case, not to mention there was some poor window washer out there, who if I didn't lock this shit down, might find himself my mid-afternoon snack.

Clinging to my humanity, my sanity, by a thread, I pushed her dark shadow back into its cage one agonizing inch at a time. My muscles locked tight with the strain of her banishment, sweat running freely between my shoulder blades.

Finally, the red haze cleared. I stood up and scrubbed a hand over my face.

Fuck no job left unresolved. Was the gratification of negotiating all the twists and turns of a difficult case, even if I emerged triumphant, worth risking my hard-won control? My body was exhausted, I wasn't sure if this job even had a resolution, and I'd nearly lapsed into full goblin. All my self-preservation instincts were screaming at me to call Rohan and tell him I couldn't do this, because I wasn't sure I'd survive.

It would be so easy to walk away. Let Drio have his happy life. I was a pro at that, telling myself a person would be happier, better off with someone else with fewer issues. Better to cut loose than be the one cut.

Sighing, I fixed the image of my blanket's silver star in my mind and peeked into the living room.

Isabella sat on the sofa. For the next several minutes, all she did was sit there, twisting her ring around and around, her face pale.

There was no sign of Drio, nor did I hear anyone else moving around.

Even if she spotted me, it would take her a moment to react. Isabella didn't know I was a half-demon—she'd just think I was an intruder and wouldn't use her magic.

Probably.

It was a chance I was willing to take. I plotted a course of action that would keep me mostly out of view behind the sofa. The most exposed bit was that first dash to the furniture, but it was only about fifteen feet.

Keeping low, I tiptoed forward.

Suddenly Isabella stiffened, her eyes rolling back and her lips moving. She wasn't making any sound and lip reading, especially in Italian, wasn't a skill set of mine. Was she reciting a spell, conversing with someone, or in a trance, speaking to herself?

Didn't matter. She was preoccupied and this was my window of opportunity. I ran for the door. Best to get to safety where I could deconstruct the situation and determine my next play.

I grabbed the door knob to the apartment. Then like an idiot, contrary to everything Greek mythology had ever taught me, I looked back.

Isabella was still mumbling, wearing that tortured facial expression and twisting the ring.

My hand tightened on the knob.

Magic artifacts were extremely rare, but they tended to follow the same principle: get it off the victim and provided they hadn't been under its influence too long, you break the compulsion. Today was Thursday and they'd been engaged since Monday night. If the ring was the problem *and* it followed the general pattern of artifact compulsion, there was a good chance that Isabella could be freed from its magic.

I could free her from its magic.

Then again, for every rule, there were a dozen exceptions when it came to demon magic and I might do more harm than good. To myself. And who's to say it was the ring anyway? Drio wasn't wearing one, and I hadn't found anything that could be a match for the ring as a compulsion artifact.

My gut twisted, instincts screaming at me that it was definitely the ring. But if she was compelled, then Drio was too, and I was no match for his years of hunter expertise. Years of training had drilled this into me: living to fight another day was much more important than heroics. I wasn't bailing on the case, just getting out of here to regroup, and come up with a new plan of attack.

Isabella whimpered.

Damn it!

She didn't even register my existence as I approached her and slowly reached for her cold, limp hand. If the ring *was* the source of the compulsion, she'd react to me touching it. If it wasn't, then she wouldn't care. I kept my eyes peeled for any reaction to my touch, but she was unresponsive.

Trying not to feel like a total perv, I ghosted my fingertip along her skin until I touched the diamond engagement ring. I was swamped with a wave of nausea and the desire to be elsewhere. The "fuck off" vibes were so strong that I had to force myself to tug on the ring.

Isabella's eyes snapped into focus. With an unholy shriek, she called up a wind that blasted me into the far wall.

I cracked my head so hard that I saw stars. It would have been nice if my spawn of a father had given me some useful defensive magic–like an energy shield or natural magic resistance, but no. Here I was, head pounding, speeding over and under blurry furniture trying not to be incinerated as Isabella whipped fireballs at me, shrieking like a harpy. Drio's happy home was rapidly becoming a lot less picturesque and a lot more post-disaster chic.

Isabella upended an ottoman in front of me. I tripped over it and smacked the photo of the gondolier, sending it crashing to the wood floor, the glass shattering in a dozen pieces. Most of the shards ended up embedded in my bare right heel when I stumbled sideways, arms up to protect myself from the barrage of books that flew at me from the shelves.

Isabella stood between me and the front door, so I leapt into the bathroom, slamming the door behind me. Before I could reach the window, no longer caring about shocking the window washer, she blew the door off its hinges. I flung myself backwards, rolling into the living room.

Magic arced over my head to burn a hole in the wall.

Her shadow loomed over me. A cruel smile spread across her face. "Demon."

Look at that. She was Drio's type after all.

I kicked her in the kneecap. Her leg buckled under her, allowing me to tackle her around the waist, and pin her to the ground. Before Isabella could take me out at close range, I slammed my fist with the reinforced ribbon into her temple.

She went slack.

I checked her pulse and breathing. Both were slow but steady. She'd recover. I sat back on my calves, breathing hard, one hand pressed to my side.

Isabella was a witch and shouldn't have sensed any demon in me. The only one who ever had was Nava when she'd been amped up on crazy levels of magic. Normal witches didn't have any kind of demon sense. Either Nava had missed a very powerful dark witch when she'd purged dark magic from the world last month, or there was a demon behind this compulsion and its magic was what had allowed Isabella to recognize my goblinness.

My gut favored the second explanation.

Grabbing a pillow, I gently placed it under Isabella's head

and eased the ring off of her finger, holding it gingerly between two fingers. When I didn't feel any ill effects from it, I wrapped it in my hair ribbon, and stuffed it in my pocket.

As a magic artifact designed to compel, the ring would leave a trace like a sticky net inside Isabella. I lay my hand on top of hers, and sent my magic inside her. Extraction was extraction, be it blood, poison, or compulsion.

There it was. Gossamer-fine magic strands blossomed out from her ring finger. I tugged on them and a brown resin flowed from her skin up through my fingers, coating my hands. Once I was satisfied that I'd gotten all of the compulsion out of her, I did a final check. All clear. I rolled the resin off my hands into a ball which I flushed down the toilet, then I turned the sink tap on hot and scrubbed until my skin was pink and raw.

The glass embedded in my feet stung and would make walking difficult in the short-term, but that was the worst of my injuries. Everything else was just scrapes. The most important thing was to replenish my energy and get out of here before Drio returned. I'd already pushed my luck. And now that I had the ring combined with the fact that Isabella was no longer compelled, maybe that would make Drio's compulsion weaker and easier to remove.

Later. I was tapped out and needed refueling stat. My stash of protein bars was in my bag, which was still in the vase in the hallway outside. Okay, Leo. All I had to do was make it to the hallway. The knocked-out witch part was handled and the twenty feet to the door seemed innocuous enough. I had this.

I did a sort of wincing hop over to the door. It opened as I was reaching for the knob, but before Drio had time to register me, I barreled past him, knocking two bags of really yummy-smelling Indian food to the ground.

Curry bled onto the floorboards.

"Fermati!" There was a loud gasp and then, "Isabella."

My heart twisted but my brain snarled that this was good. She'd provide the distraction so I could hole up somewhere safe

46

and recharge. I flung the large vase over and grabbed my messenger bag and coat. Running on fumes, I thundered toward the stairs, expecting to be grabbed by Speedy Gonzales at any moment.

Swearing more than Samuel L. Jackson on that plane thanks to the damn glass, I hopped the stairs three at a time, crashing down onto the second-floor landing and rounding the railing to take the final flight of stairs.

Every bloody footprint was an exercise in agony, but freedom was in sight. Right now, I was weak. Easy pickings. But I was very good at hiding. I just needed to get outside.

Coasting on icy panic and fumes, I leapt off the final few stairs. I'd done it. Soon as I got through this door, I could disappear into the streets of Rome. Exhilaration flooded my veins and gave me one last burst of speed to zip across the foyer and grab the handle to the building's exterior.

I was yanked backward by the strap of my messenger bag.

Drio slammed the door shut, the bustling piazza vanished, and with it, any hope of escape.

5

As a half-demon, I had a kill spot.

As a Rasha, Drio had a reputation for being thorough. And okay, he'd been pretty thorough as not-a-Rasha also, a fact my body hummed remembering. Argh. Not the time. My eyes bounced around the foyer, but there was nowhere to hide and no point in running. He'd just catch me.

I slammed the door shut on the memory of a very different night he'd caught me. Given the flat look on Drio's face, this situation didn't have that multiple orgasm feel.

Mentally cataloguing everything in my bag, I inched my hand under its top flap. P.I. rule number four: always have a way to make it out alive. If I could just reach my lock pick, it would be sharp enough to use as a weapon. "Is this how it ends?"

"Che cosa? What are you doing here?"

Eyes narrowing, I closed my hand around the lock pick. "You remember who I am?"

"Leonie Hendricks."

"And I'm what?"

"A half-demon." Of all the things he could have said, he was certainly quick with the one response that marked us as enemies. He didn't recognize me as a threat, though.

How insulting. You'd think this compelled Rasha, of all people, could at least try and kill me. I swallowed a bitter laugh. "What else?"

"A student."

"And?" Huh, that was kind of growly.

"Part-time P.I."

"Three strikes, you're out," I said. "Now, if you'll excuse me—"

He stuck out a hand. "What am I missing? You're Nava's best friend. What's wrong? Did something happen to her and Ro?"

I rolled the lock pick in my hand. Jugular or femoral? Both excellent bleed-out veins. No, prison orange would clash with my red hair.

"They're fine. I'm just here to, you know," I mashed my lips into what may have resembled a smile if you were extremely near-sighted or socially obtuse, "congratulate you on your engagement. So, congrats! And later."

Hefting my bag on my shoulder, I wrenched the front building door open. I wasn't bailing on the job, but I needed to formulate my next move and I couldn't do it with the sight and smell of him scrambling my synapses. Plus, my heel was killing me, I had to find some First Aid stuff, maybe shove some pins into a blond-haired, green-eyed voodoo doll.

"Don't go," Drio blurted out in a panicked voice and grabbed me.

I chopped his hand off of my shoulder. "Why not?"

Screw the niceties, I needed food. I ate two chocolate chip cookie dough flavored protein bars that stuck in my throat, while Drio stood there, face twitching, figuring out how to answer. It made me want to punch him. This wasn't a hard question.

Compulsion or not, everything else about him was normal. He knew my name and that I was Nava's best friend, he could probably describe my apartment in perfect detail. He'd just conveniently lost the one piece of information that mattered most—that I was the woman he'd declared his feeling for in such an over-the-top way that it had gone viral—and I didn't have it in me to be the bigger person. My goblin had come out when I'd seen him with Isabella and he couldn't even remember what I meant to him.

"You're…" He stretched out his hand like he was about to caress my cheek, then dropped his hand at his side. Confusion flitted over his face.

He doesn't want you to go even if he doesn't know why. Something's up. You going to walk away or are you going to fight for this? Hope, that fickle bitch, had almost been my undoing with him before. How dare she show her brazen self once more, taunting me?

Professionally, I'd see this through because if I didn't, the magic would only continue to sink its hooks deeper, causing him to fall harder and harder for Isabella, who would probably reject him. It could propel him into stalker territory with a bad ending for both of them.

But what did I want in terms of the two of us? I swallowed the last of my bar, ready to "Ciao, bello" out of his life on a personal level. I could be with someone who didn't make me go all Mr. Hyde. Drio had pulled the grandest of gestures, and then peaced out on me. What if the moment he came to his senses, he ran away out of fear? This wouldn't be the first time he did a one-eighty on us.

I sighed. Work first.

"You've been compelled," I said. "Hand me the nice artifact you were given."

He blinked at me with only slightly more understanding than a slack-jawed yokel. Drio was many things, but he wasn't stupid. He had no recollection of any artifact. There had to be one, however, since Isabella had definitely been under the influence of the ring and not a direct verbal order.

"It always has to be the hard way with you, doesn't it?" I did a quick scan. No shirt pockets, no visible jewelry. I lunged at him, worming my fingers into the front pockets of his jeans.

Drio fought me, trying to pull my hands out, but he could only blame himself for fashionably tight pockets.

The right one was empty but in the left one, I touched a tiny bar of iron about as long and thick as my thumb, and almost blacked out because it was brimming with demon magic.

Drio grabbed my throat and I went still.

"Give me the iron bar, Drio." This would be a good time to worry about him killing me instead of feeling pathetically happy that he was touching me.

His body vibrated with tension, every muscle locked tight. Drio was strong-willed and maybe this was his struggle to resist the compulsion and give me the bar, but it was equally as likely that this was the build-up to my chalk outline gracing the tile floor. Or rather, the pile of gold dust that all half-demons turned into when killed. Damn it, I didn't want to end up in a vacuum cleaner.

I barely dared to breathe, my eyes locked on his. "Let go."

He made a sound of distress and unlocked his fingers from my throat, his hand shaking and his olive skin a ghastly white. "Get away from me."

"No."

"Leonie." My name was a plea on his lips.

"You're not going to hurt me, so shut up and give me the iron bar."

Anger flashed in the depths of his green eyes. Anger was good, because it meant I was annoying his regular self, but it was all too quickly replaced with a bleak hopelessness.

I lay my hand on his cheek. "I'm here."

"Take it," he whispered.

I skimmed my fingers over the iron bar, but he held himself in check. He was really trusting me to help him, so I snatched the bar away.

Drio crashed to his knees, gripping his head with a roar.

I shoved the iron bar and the ring in my messenger bag and tossed the bag to the far end of the foyer. My coat slid to the ground.

"Hold still." I grabbed his shoulders.

Isabella had been unconscious when I'd removed the ring, which was a blessing. I didn't have that luxury with Drio, but time was of the essence. I had to get that compulsion out of him before he became unstable. Well, more unstable than usual for him, which was saying a lot.

A milky film rolled over his eyes and he lashed out at me, nailing me with a sweeping kick to the same poor thigh that had recently sustained the injury from the asper.

Part of me was impressed because damn, he was on his knees and that was incredibly hot.

The rest of me screamed "fuuuuck!" and grabbed the ceramic planter to the left of the staircase, overflowing with oversized fronds. I winged it at him.

He flashed out of its way. Greenery flew through the air and the planter cracked into two large pieces as it hit the tile.

Drio grabbed me.

I bit the fleshy part of his palm. When that didn't release his hold, I kicked him between the legs. He doubled over with a moan, allowing me to jump on his back like a monkey. With only the tiniest bit of guilt for his pain, I wrapped my hands around his neck, the only bare flesh I could access, and drew out the brown sticky resin, while he remained bent in half and breathing heavily from the agony of being kicked in the nuts.

After a few moments, Drio relaxed under my touch.

Satisfied I had all of the compulsion, I slid off his back, uttering another curse when my poor glass-imbedded heel hit the tile. "You're welcome, you big jerk."

Drio turned to face me, still ashen. "You kicked me in the balls. Call it even."

"Get engaged again and lose them entirely."

He rubbed his forehead. "We were compelled."

"Demon should have done its homework. Isabella's too nice for you."

He wrapped my ponytail around his finger and tugged me close. "These past few days? I thought you were a dream."

"No kidding? I thought you were a dick."

He barked a laugh. "No doubt."

"We should get back upstairs." I turned away from him to retrieve my bag, but he caught my arm. The clean one, not the one with the gross resin hardening into an itchy amber.

"Leonie." Damn him and his sexy Italian-accented English. He didn't get to just ignore everything that had happened and turn those half-lidded eyes on me like sex missiles.

"What?"

"Thank you."

"I'll add it to your bill," I said.

"I prefer not to run a tab." He stepped closer. "Settle up for services rendered?"

There would be no "settling" of squat because this roller coaster car had officially jumped the tracks.

Except... there was that light of his attention, shining down on me like a galaxy of stars. One last kiss couldn't hurt. A single smooch to relive on cold nights.

I nodded, the tiniest of motions, yet it sent me into freefall.

Drio cupped my face and brushed his lips against mine.

The world fell away under his soft, sweet teasing.

His hands skimmed down my sides. My sweater had risen up and the naked press of his fingertips against my hipbones made me shiver. The intensity of his grip was at odds with the languid exploration of this kiss.

Gold glitter replaced the blood in my veins, swirling like confetti on New Year's Eve in Times Square. I clutched his waistband, needing an anchor to keep me from floating away. His kiss whispered to the parts of me I'd kept hidden. *I see you. I'm with you.*

I rose higher on tiptoe, melting.

He sucked on my lower lip, and my mind blanked.

The happy fun cage deathtrap rumbled down to our floor, the elevator door creaking open.

"Scusami," a man said and brushed past us out the building door.

Drio groaned and pulled away. His fingers flexed against my skin. He took a slow, deep breath. "This wasn't how I planned our first decent kiss."

"Improv worked." I straightened my clothes with shaky fingers, and winced.

Drio scooped me up into his arms.

"What are you doing?" I flailed my dirty hand above my head.

"Your foot is covered in blood. It needs to be cleaned and treated. And do something for that arm because that shit you pulled out of me is nasty. I don't want it sitting on you."

I wasn't used to people taking care of me. People loved me. That was all good. But care for me? My mom was kind of a scatterbrain. Nava would give her life for me, but part of why we liked each other so much as friends was because we respected the other's self-sufficiency. And Harry's brand of love was to make sure I could handle anything, like the time he paid off security staff to get us in to a skyscraper under construction and forced me to walk girders high above the city every night for a week to overcome my fear of heights. Thus, why his recent hovering was so disconcerting.

"Put me down." I pushed against Drio and he eased me to the floor. "I'm not some helpless female."

"Right. The first word that comes to mind with you. Followed by 'sweet-tempered' and 'accommodating.'"

I hopped forward. "Carrying me doesn't imply a lot of faith in my ability to take care of myself, plus you didn't even try to kill me when you saw me."

Drio twitched like his brain was short-circuiting. His fingers curled into throttle mode.

"Happy to remedy that now," he snapped and stormed off toward the stairs. He made it halfway up the first flight before turning. "Are you coming upstairs to get fixed up?"

"I dunno. What's the magic word?"

"Impossible? Infuriating? Isabella." He swore. Then he held out his hand. "Leonie, please."

I limped over to my messenger bag, slung it over my shoulder, and grabbed my coat. "Might as well. I need to interview both of you and there's no time like the present."

His eyes widened to comic proportions. "I'm a job?"

"Yes. One I'd like to resolve as quickly as possible. My client hired me to find out what had happened to you. This is strictly a professional visit."

"Keep telling yourself that, bella. Who's the client? Nava?" He shot me a grin so wolfish that my stomach did two and half somersaults.

Feeling like Little Red Riding Hood alone in the dark forest, I tamped down the urge to taunt, "Here, wolfie, wolfie," then run and see if he'd chase me. "Like Nee could afford me. And I'm not saying. My clients are a matter of confidentiality."

"Rohan, then." Drio jogged down the stairs and relieved me of my coat and bag. "Would you have come anyway?"

"Maybe. But only to stab you."

He laughed, a rich belly laugh.

I rolled onto the insides of my feet, then winced again.

Drio slung the bag over his shoulder and waited.

"Fine. You may carry me."

"Grazie, principessa. I appreciate you bestowing this favor upon me." He lifted me into his arms and flashed up the stairs.

"For the record," I said, when we reached his floor and the world eased back into focus. "Your sarcasm is going to get you punched in the throat one day. Try being more pleasant. Like me. Also, stop with the princess nonsense. I'm your full-on queen."

He rolled his eyes.

We entered his apartment and I let out a soft gasp, because the place was pristine. Isabella must have done some witchy restoration deal. Other than the artwork that was stacked in a neat pile instead of on the walls, there wasn't a single sign that any damage had ever occurred.

Isabella sat on the sofa, hunched into herself pathetically. A bruise bloomed along her temple.

"Shit. I'm sorry." I wriggled out of Drio's hold, jumping across the room. "Ow. Ow. Ow."

"Madonna mia," Drio muttered. He sat down next to Isabella, tossing my bag and coat on a chair. "How do you feel?"

I went into the bathroom and scrubbed the resin off. I had to pry it off in places with my fingernails where it had hardened into a shell.

"Woozy." Isabella spoke with a lilting Italian accent.

"Follow my finger," Drio said. There was silence for a moment. "You'll be okay."

I dried my clean hands and returned to the living room.

"Who are you and why are you sorry?" Isabella touched her head. "Did you do this?"

"Yes, and I feel terrible, but I had to free you." I held out my hand and she shook it. "I'm Leonie Hendricks. I'm here in a private investigator capacity. My firm does a lot of work involving demons, and I discovered that you were compelled by something with powerful magic."

She blinked at me. "*You're* a demon. I remember knowing that for some reason."

"Half-demon, and I suspect it was part of the compulsion." I tried not to fidget under her stare, but she studied me so intently that I got nervous. "I wasn't the one who compelled you."

She snapped her fingers, her smile lighting up her entire face. "The video! That's why you look familiar. You're Drio's girl-friend." Her hand flew to her mouth. "This suddenly got very awkward."

I swallowed. "Girlfriend? No, it's far too early for formal

titles." *Girlfriend* hadn't been on the original "slow and smart" plan for at least another three or four months. I'd been dragged into the spotlight a week ago, and now everyone seemed to expect me to be settling in for the long haul. I needed time and space to think. Not be a flourish on some viral news story.

Drio crossed his arms and leveled me with a stare.

I leveled it right back. It was all fine and good that he wanted to be official, but he was also the one who messed up by dumping me and blowing up at me and then not making up for a long time. And then he went to Italy and got his stupid ass compelled. He didn't get to be the wounded party here.

"Regardless, I punched you so you wouldn't fry me, not because you were engaged to my…" I pointed at Drio. "Him."

"Him" snorted.

Isabella said a few words in Italian to Drio in a very stern voice. He replied to her with something that took her aback.

"You were going to stab him?" she said.

"You make my decision sound so past tense."

Drio grinned at me. "I dare you."

She nodded, not at all fazed that this passed for foreplay between Drio and me. "Va bene. You took the ring, didn't you?"

"I did. And a small bar of iron I found on Drio. The ring caused your compulsion and the bar caused his, but usually there's a connection between items used on multiple targets."

"It's an ancient Italian custom," Isabella said. "Bridegrooms carry a small piece of iron in their pocket to symbolize the strength of a couple's commitment."

"It's not an engagement tradition," Drio said. "It happens on the wedding day itself. Any self-respecting Italian, even a demonic one, would know that." He shook his head disapprovingly.

"Incorrect adherence to tradition? That's your problem here?" I said.

"It's sloppy," he said. "It's not an Italian demon or witch behind this."

"Unless that's what they want you think. I'm not ready to rule anyone out." I took a deep breath. "Not even Antonia."

Isabella practically shot out of her seat. "Nonna would never do this. Drio, tell her."

He nodded. "She hates Rasha. There's no motivation for her to put Isabella and me together. It's not Antonia."

I pulled out my phone and started dialing.

"Who are you calling?" he said.

I blinked up innocently at him. "Harry. I have a couple other open cases you might like to explain to me. I'm going to have him email you the files."

A muscle ticked in his jaw. "That won't be necessary."

I shot him a bland smile and put my phone down. "I agree it's unlikely, however, at the moment, she's the strongest link between the two of you. She's held her position for fifty years so her magic must be very powerful, and as an Italian woman, she'd be well aware of the tradition and the fact that the objects were closely related enough to be harmonious compulsion artifacts."

Drio looked like he had a snappy comeback for that but was spared my wrath by his door literally blowing open.

"Isabella Aria De Luca!" An old woman in a shapeless black dress and thick black stockings stood in the doorway. Her over-sized head with its gray helmet-like hair bobbed on her wrinkly, skinny body, and her stare could frighten children.

I pressed back into the couch cushions. Sure, I wasn't a child, but I'd filled my quota on dangerous witch encounters for today, so why push my luck and call attention to myself?

Isabella eeped. "Nonna."

Antonia's eyes narrowed in on Drio. "And you."

Before Drio had managed to rise fully off the sofa, let alone run out of the danger zone, which despite Kenny Loggins's enthusiasm was not a good place to be, Antonia had flash-frozen Drio inside a block of ice.

So much for Ro's claim that old ladies liked Drio.

6

What did you get when you mixed two very angry witches, one half-goblin, and a mystery that needed a convenient scapegoat? Apparently, one Rasha popsicle and a very bad situation for me, the half-demon who no longer had anyone to vouch for me being on their side. The smart part of me was understandably nervous, but I'd be lying if part of me didn't take in the jut of Antonia's chin, as immutable in her ways as my own grandmère had been, and think, "Okay lady, Bring it."

So much for staying under the radar.

I knocked on the ice block that dripped water onto the tiles. "Is this really necessary?"

"*Nonna.*" Isabella flicked her fingers at Drio and the ice transformed back into water, splooshing all over the foyer and soaking my feet.

Drio was shivering. His hair was plastered along the sides of his face and he was snorting and coughing.

Isabella used her elimination magic to get rid of all of the water. At least Drio was now in dry clothes, though his lips were still blue.

I ran into his bathroom and grabbed the lone towel hanging on a hook, wincing under my breath at the glass in my foot, while

Isabella yelled at her grandmother in rapid Italian. Staying well out of hand jab range so I didn't lose an eye, I helped Drio wrap himself in it because his fingers were shaking too hard to grasp the cloth.

How had I ended up playing Florence Nightingale while the witches engaged in some terminal nearsightedness about which of them was more at fault, rather than the actual danger we faced? Was I the only professional here?

Antonia crossed her arms, a mulish expression on her face. The door slammed behind her, but sadly she was still on this side of it. "What did you do to my granddaughter?"

"Nothing," Drio said. Still shivering, he leaned into me. I scooted closer to rub some circulation back into his arms.

Isabella glared at me. "Still believe Nonna was behind the compulsion?"

Antonia rounded on me. "Ma, che sei grullo?"

Drio chuckled, but dropped his eyes to his feet under her glower.

Would have been nice if he'd filled me in on what was so funny, because right now I was feeling like I'd entrusted my life to a flaky Google Translate and shit was about to hit the fan. "I don't speak Ital—"

"They were compelled and you thought I would…" Ice magic crackled along Antonia's hands.

I scooted backwards. I'd already seen what happened with Captain Ice Cube. I had no desire to try it myself.

"Who's your coven leader?" Antonia said.

"No coven," I said.

"You're a rogue?" She advanced on me.

"I'm not a witch." I grabbed a heavy coffee-table book and got ready to swing.

Drio blocked her way. His color was better and his shivering had subsided, but his shoulders still had a weary set to them and his fingertips were blue. "Don't touch her," he said in a quietly menacing voice.

Isabella tugged on her grandmother's sleeve. "Leonie broke the compulsion."

Antonia shut down her magic and sat down next to her granddaughter. "How? She just admitted she's not a witch."

I set the book down. You'd think that after having done this with my friends, Drio, and the Rasha-witch coalition that telling people what I was would get easier. But no, it was like coming out over and over again and always hoping for the best. "I'm a half-redcap."

Antonia's expression froze into revulsion. She took Isabella's arm and sent a soft orb of healing magic into her. "You let her use magic on you?"

My hands tightened into fists. "You let her go to your house and get compelled?"

Isabella elbowed her grandmother, shooting me a look of apology.

Drio leaned back against his sofa cushions, one arm stretched out behind me, and the towel still wrapped over his shoulders. "Leonie got it out. She's good. You have nothing to worry about."

A glow spread through me, but I stayed professional and did not grin goofily.

Antonia probed for any traces a moment longer, then dropped her magic. "Tolerable for a half-demon."

And that's all I'd ever be to many in the magical community. A half-demon. Almost bad enough to kill on sight, but not quite. I'd done a great job getting these two dummies uncompelled and I didn't even warrant a thank-you.

"How can you sit here next to her when your job is to rid the world of demons?" Antonia demanded.

Drio's eyes hardened. "My job is to rid the world of evil. You'd do well to understand the difference."

Antonia looked unconvinced.

"I was in the plaza in Jerusalem when Gog and Magog were

set loose," I said. "Were you there fighting? Because I don't remember seeing you."

Antonia grew stonier.

Ha. Point: me. "I'm also part of the team that is building the information system for witches and Rasha and I was integral in getting access to the demon dark web. I've survived Malik, now Satan, and nightmares you can't even begin to conceive of, and I'm your best hope of finding out who's behind all this, precisely because of what I am."

"Part goblin," she said.

"No. Damn good at my job." I smiled thinly. "I don't give a flying fuck if you like me, but if you want this handled, you will respect me."

Antonia waved a hand at me. "Impress me with your brilliance." The smile she gave me had a dangerous edge. "Then I will decide."

This woman was not to be underestimated. Well, neither was I.

Drio headed into the kitchen and rummaged around in a cupboard. He turned on the tap, letting the water run.

"First, we build a timeline of events. Walk me through everything you can remember." I pulled out my phone and opened the recording app. "Drio, you need to be part of this."

"Aspetta." He carried out a basin of water, steam rising off of it. Under one arm was a small First Aid kit. Setting the basin on the table, he pulled out a dripping washcloth and wrung it out. He handed it to Isabella, who dabbed at the dried blood on her head.

"Who did that?" Antonia demanded.

"I don't remember. It happened during the compulsion." Props for the steely glint in Isabella's eyes that matched the steel in her spine.

Antonia let it go.

Drio handed me a pair of tweezers. "Get the glass out of your foot while we do this."

I hit play on the recorder. "Thursday, October 10. Interview with Antonia D'Amico, Isabella De Luca, and Drio Rossi."

With her bruise now clean, Isabella quickly healed it.

I twisted my foot around to get at the glass. "Drio. Start with how you got involved."

"My mother called me a few nights before Ro's concert asking if I'd do her a favor. An old friend of hers, Rafaella, had a daughter who was a witch and wanted to train as a hunter but her mother, Antonia, head of the coven, was blocking the idea." He shot her a pointed look.

Antonia shrugged. "Let the Rasha fight demons and die. That's all they're good for anyway."

Drio lost his temper, laying into her in Italian. Antonia's reply was just as heated. They ran roughshod over Isabella's tentative attempts to disarm the conversation.

I whistled loudly. "Enough. Lose the alpha attitudes and play nice. I don't know who or what we're facing, so you're going to save your issues for later and not undermine me or my investigation. Got it?"

Antonia and Drio stared at me with identical mutinous expressions.

"I didn't hear you." I jabbed the tweezers at them.

They mumbled their assent.

"Why do you hate Rasha so much?" I winced, pulling out a tiny piece of glass.

"It's not relevant," Antonia said.

"It is if that's why these two were targeted."

Antonia stared at me, refusing to answer.

"You literally just agreed not to hamper the investigation."

The pigheaded old witch didn't budge.

I worked unsuccessfully at another glass sliver. Drio caught my foot, taking the tweezers away from me.

"I've got this." I glared at him and yanked my foot away.

"If you can't walk or your foot gets infected, then who's hampering the investigation?"

Oh, he didn't.

I was beyond done: with these witches, this investigation, and most of all with Drio being so… Drio. France. I could move to my grandmother's homeland. It's pretty and even better, it wasn't teeming with irritating Italians and their high-handed opinions.

"If you're so concerned," I said, "you could ask if I needed help instead of charging in."

Isabella smacked Drio. "Leonie's right. You took over because she wasn't doing things fast enough or your way, when she's the only reason either of us are thinking clearly."

"You wouldn't treat Rohan this way," I said. "You're not being professional."

Antonia did this combo eye roll, huff, and snort that conveyed at this point there was little Drio or I could to lower her opinion of us. "You." She pointed to Drio. "Ask first. You." She pointed at me. "Let him help. This is taking all day."

Drio's jaw was tight. "Mi dispiace. Do you need help?"

Fine. Let this go faster. I set my foot in his lap and tossed him the tweezers.

He angled my heel toward the light. With featherlight touches, he pulled the slivers of glass from my skin. His fingers were warm and strong, his movements confident and his touch gentle.

I cleared my throat. "Antonia, why did you agree to see Drio?"

"Because Mama and I fought to give Drio a chance to present his case." Isabella cut in. "I really want to hunt and I really want Nonna's blessing. I couldn't live being estranged from her. My father died when I was a baby and she and Mama are my entire family."

Antonia's expression softened and she smiled at her grand-daughter. "I live in a very rural area and my neighbors are quite a distance away. I said I'd hear him out but I was coming to Rome the next day to stay with my daughter and he'd have to leave then."

Drio ran a finger over my foot. It was a clinical examination to check for glass, but my nerve endings lit up like a pinball machine and I couldn't help the tiny shiver as I pulled my foot away.

There was a universe where he was gallant enough not to smirk at my reaction. This was not that universe.

"Did you have the iron bar and the ring at this point?" I wrung out the second washcloth and cleaned my foot.

Drio disinfected the tweezers and replaced them in the First Aid kit. "No."

"And it was just you and Antonia that night?"

"Yes," Antonia said.

"My advisor had asked me to accompany her to a conference in Geneva," Isabella said. "When I returned, I planned to go to Nonna's place for a few days for some downtime."

"Antonia listened." Drio opened the kit and handed me a tube of topical ointment. "But she didn't budge on her position and I figured that was that. The next day—"

"This is October 1, correct?" I cleaned my other foot as well, since my sole was black with dirt.

"Yes," Drio said. "Antonia drove out ahead of me, but when I got to the end of the property, a sudden storm kicked up out of nowhere and a bolt of lightning knocked an old tree into my path. That's when all the fuckery started. I got out of the car and was lashed with wind so strong, I couldn't move. I managed to turn the car around and get back to the house when a snow-storm buried the place in minutes. I couldn't open the doors or the windows to go outside, and neither my cell phone nor the landline worked."

"It wasn't a compulsion at this point," I said. "Any reports of odd weather patterns?"

"Not that I heard," Antonia said. "There was no mention of

any freak storm on the weather channels and none of our neighbors called about anything unusual."

"The snow wasn't there when I arrived on the eighth, either," Isabella added.

"A demon who can manipulate weather," I said. "There's a number of those. That seems most likely, but so as not to rule anything out at this point, I imagine certain witches are good at weather manipulation as well and, Antonia, your dislike of Rasha is well-known. This could be payback against you. Tangling Isabella and Drio up in an engagement you'd be sure to hate. Not to mention any other agenda attached to it. Will you give me a list of those who might want to harm you?"

Shock and displeasure flashed across her face. "There are only two women who are that powerful and hold a grudge. One lost her magic to Gog and Magog and the other is… incapacitated."

Isabella made a slashing motion across her throat.

Wide-eyed, I flicked my gaze at Antonia.

Isabella gave me the tiniest nod.

Fucking hell.

7

I stumbled over the last part of the conversation to find where I'd left off. "A demon then. It wanted you there," I said to Drio.

"It got me. I was trapped." His voice iced over. "One week. The snow didn't melt. By the end I was foraging in the cellar for questionable canned goods."

Isabella shook her head sadly. "You weren't some random element. Whoever is behind this targeted you specifically."

"You as Rasha, or you as Drio?" I applied the topical ointment to my foot and then snagged a pair of socks from my bag and put them on. The throbbing was already dying down.

"I'm betting the former." Drio drummed his fingers against his thigh. "But why?"

"Having a hunter under its control would be a coup." I wiggled my clean, warm toes. It felt marvelous.

"Having both a hunter and a witch is even better," Isabella said. "The demon doing this gets two powerful beings that it can control."

"Yes and no," I said. "There are two ways a person can be compelled: either by a direct verbal command or a magic artifact. Each has its pros and cons."

"The verbal command is stronger," Drio said. "But most demons can only sustain it for a short time."

"Look at you, smarty pants," I said.

"I'm not just a pretty face." He tapped his head. "Keen mind, trained in multiple disciplines."

"Uh-huh." Obviously, he was smart. I wouldn't have given him a chance otherwise. Hot dude in and of itself held very little appeal for me except for a one-night ride. "Verbal compulsions are best used to force someone to carry out a specific action within a specific timeframe. Luckily for humans, there aren't many demons who can verbally compel."

"Not anymore," Drio said. "On behalf of the Brotherhood, you're welcome."

Isabella hid a smile. Not very well. "This wasn't verbal, it was a ring and an iron bar."

"Right," I said. "That's the other way. A magic artifact. This method is more of a slow burn. An artifact's compulsion builds up over time, leaving the target more and more under its thrall. In theory, this is a great system. The behavior of the compelled person can be manipulated months or even years down the road. Think of it like a very gradual personality change. Gift a well-known liberal politician on the upswing of their career with some amulet, and by the time they become president, your evil way of thinking is their evil way of thinking."

Antonia threw me a considering look. Yeah, I knew my shit, lady.

"That's why I don't believe the engagement was the end game," I said. "They were working up to something else with you two."

"Artifacts sound like the better option for a compulsion," Isabella said.

"I wasn't kidding about the 'in theory' part," I said. "Long-term magic compulsions come with high rates of insanity."

Isabella shuddered.

"Who knew you were supposed to go to your Nonna's?" I said.

"My mother and my grandmother." Isabella's hand flew to her mouth. "Madonna mia. Does Mama know?"

"Everyone knows," Antonia said sourly.

"But she doesn't know from me. I let my phone die. Which I never do." Isabella went into Drio's bedroom.

I blinked. Her stuff was in his bedroom. She'd slept in his bed. In the chaos of learning about his engagement, it hadn't occurred to me what else might have happened.

Drio attempted to catch my eye, but I twisted away from him, re-arranging the First Aid kit while I spoke to Antonia. "I only have a few more questions. This is all important information which I'm going to use to compile a list of demon types who fit the profile."

Isabella returned with her cell phone which she plugged in. It went off with a flurry of notification chimes. She held the phone like it was a live cobra and stuffed it under a couch cushion. "I can't deal with this yet."

Weird, because I couldn't deal with the idea of her sleeping with Drio, even if compelled, yet either.

"Let's get back to the ring." Oh good, my voice didn't waver. "How did you get it?"

Drio took the First Aid kit away. "The ring and iron bar appeared in my room Monday night. Soon after Isabella arrived."

"That's when you asked her to marry you?" I screwed my P.I. brain on tight. I'd heard worse. Like the demon who'd described in enthusiastic detail skinning and eating a toddler. This didn't even rate.

I tore off a cuticle.

Isabella leaned over and squeezed my hand. "This can't be easy to hear."

"All good. I need to know for the job. The proposal?"

Drio gave me an inscrutable look before he answered. "I

picked up the bar and gave Isabella the ring, but I didn't actually ask. It just became a thing."

The fact that he hadn't actually spoken the words, even under a compulsion, made this miserable situation a little easier to bear. The way that being pinned under a car that at least hadn't burst into flame was easier to bear.

"How did you find out you could leave?" I said.

"We had to come plan the wedding," Isabella said.

Drio swore. "We better cancel the planner before she starts booking things."

"And you so wanted that matching china." I shot Drio a mock frown.

A vein in Drio's neck throbbed.

"Basta!" Antonia stood up. "I've heard enough."

"I'll deal with the wed-uh, cancellation stuff and get my things." Lunging for her phone, Isabella bolted into Drio's room.

"I'm going to find out who did this and why," I said. "Are you going to stand in my way?"

Antonia shot me a cool look. "You are a halfling and you are only capable of so much. You have some skill. You're reasonably intelligent. But if you put Isabella in danger for one second, you will pay."

She touched her index finger to her eye and then jabbed it at me twice. Did she just threaten to curse me? Seriously? I was billing Rohan for danger pay.

In the face of Italian witch curses, the smart thing to do would be to walk away on the technicality that I'd done the job I'd been hired for—discovered what had happened to them. They'd been compelled, end of story. But I'd never be able to look myself in the eye again if I didn't totally unravel this mystery. I had to know the answer to the puzzle, because it was gnawing at me and my sleuthing instincts were tingling to get to the bottom of this.

Hell, yeah, I was invested.

For sure there would be more danger ahead and Antonia

would blame me in some horrifically painful way, but I wasn't going to quit.

No job left unresolved. And this wasn't just a job. It was Drio and it was Isabella, and I was damned if some hellspawn was going to toy with either of them.

"Still not going anywhere," I said.

Antonia did the finger eye jab thing to Drio as well, bellowed for Isabella, and swept out of the apartment.

Isabella scrambled after her. "Leonie?" She toyed with the handle of her suitcase. "Nonna's adoptive father was a Rasha and he was a horrible person. He would only let her use her magic for healing."

"Women's magic." I sneered.

Isabella's eyes flashed. "Sì. Hunting was for men, and all other magic was pointless to him. Her mother, Francesca, protested. Nonna's being a witch had caught them by surprise, but once she got over the shock, Francesca wanted to find someone to help Nonna develop her power. My great-grandfather decided otherwise."

She bit her lip, looking out the window.

"It didn't go well," I said softly.

She shook her head. "He was physically abusive and when he wasn't around, he had other Rasha keep an eye on her. Nonna was forced to hide her magic until she was old enough and powerful enough to leave home and go somewhere he couldn't touch her."

"The Brotherhood of David, misogynist dicks since 1000 BCE. Thank you for telling me."

"No, grazie. I know you'll find the demon." She kissed me on both cheeks, waved at Drio and ran after Antonia.

Nice woman. Hope her grandmother didn't curse me. I clicked off the recording app, picked up the basin and the used washcloths, and marched into the kitchen.

Drio followed me. "Nothing happened."

"So certain of that, are you?"

"I remember everything." He rubbed the back of his neck. "It was like a dream, like it was playing out in someone else's life and I couldn't change things, but I do know what happened."

"Then why didn't you know I was your 'girlfriend?'" I totally used air quotes.

"I don't know," he said. "Unless that was part of what made the compulsion work. Forgetting that you were in my life. That won't ever happen again. You're too important."

I dumped the water down the drain. "You know, it would be nice not to be jumped around at warp speed to whatever stage of our relationship you deem appropriate. You were trapped and you were compelled and I don't blame you for that part, but fuck, Drio. I haven't had a minute to feel comfortable about where I stand with you, so it's nice that nothing happened, but emotionally, I'm still about five steps behind you and I'm reeling."

Drio took the basin away–I'd been clutching it like a shield–and dropped it on the counter with a clatter. "I'll do anything to make it up to you. But I swear, compelled or not, I slept on the sofa. I had this deep sense that doing anything, even just sleeping next to her would be wrong." He took my hands. "It was because of you. You may have been a dream, but you were here. In my heart. Even magic can't break that."

"Stop." I jerked my hands away. "Enough of these grand declarations. You're overcompensating because you feel guilty. Well, I absolve you."

I mimed tapping him on the shoulder with a wand and stormed into the living room, but he failed to get my stompy hint to give me some space, and followed me.

"Keep your absolution," he said. "I'm good."

"No, you're not. If you had just met some woman that you liked you wouldn't treat her the way you've treated me." I crouched down to rummage through my bag, not having any clue what I was looking for, but wanting to look busy as I turned my back to him.

"I was an asshole when I found out about you," he said.

"I don't mean that. Yeah, your behavior back then was awful, but given what happened with Asha, I get it." In a move that should have gotten me sainthood, I passed over the lock pick in favor of another protein bar. That's right, Leo. Eat the nice food and stop engaging because this conversation was going nowhere good.

Drio pinched the bridge of his nose. "Then what do you mean? Because I'm trying here, but I'm lost."

I crushed the bar in my fist before I got in my first bite. "It means I didn't need a damn song in front of a packed room that ended up all over the internet. It means I didn't need to be the one who, according to the paparazzi, 'you'd moved on from' when this engagement hit the papers. And it means I don't need your 'being in your heart because magic can't break that' bullshit. Like that 'cuore mio,' 'my heart,' crap you gave me after the song. You don't love me, Drio. You don't know me well enough yet and I don't know you."

Mushed chocolate mint energy bar glooped through my fingers where I'd squeezed it too hard. I scowled at it. Way to go, self.

Drio caught my wrist and hauled me back to the kitchen. He cleaned off my hand with a rag, scrubbing surprisingly gently given his angry silence, then pitched it in the sink. "I finally sort my shit out and you're telling me I'm wrong because you don't think you deserve to be loved, is that it?"

I winced. "It's not that. I just don't want to get caught up in a fairy tale that won't last."

"Do you want us to last?" He raked a hand through his hair. "Or is the better question do you want us to begin?"

Yes. Not just for sex, though yes please and more, but for him. He was smart and funny and driven by passion. Those qualities were hugely attractive, especially his passion, but he lived it at this all-or-nothing level and I'd been naïve to assume that could change. My life could never be all-or-nothing because my "all" included my goblin. And I could never let a monster like her run free.

Drio inspired the same volatile feelings in me that I did in him. But he could surf those waves. I'd be pulled under and drown.

Also, he was hella bossy.

We stood in a loaded, miserable silence for a few moments. Drio swore under his breath, then crowded up into my space, bracketing his hands on the cabinet behind my head. "I'm going to say this once, and once only, capisci?"

I could have easily ducked free, but I was curious and he was hot, so I nodded.

"After Asha died, I lived with guilt for years. I drank from it more than any bottle and I let it poison me. Whatever I've said or done to you? These grand fucking declarations? They weren't out of guilt. They were and are because for the first time in years I feel like someone truly sees me, all of me, and I'm not out here drowning in the cold, dark depths. You've lit up my world, Leonie Hendricks, and much as my cynical little heart barely beats, you make it race. So, I will take us as fast or as slow as you want to because I don't want some fairy tale garbage either. But don't ever tell me that anything good I feel for you comes from guilt. Nothing good comes from that, and you are everything."

Everything including being a monster.

My goblin's eyes blinked open with a smug satisfied gleam, watching and waiting.

Being with Drio could cost me everything.

But, so could being without him.

Rock, meet hard place. Other women got to feel jealous or insecure and it was just emotions. For me, they became a literal fight with my inner demon and if that part of me finally won, I'd be lost for good.

Could I do this?

You don't get to win, I said.

She smirked. *We'll see.*

He rested his hands on my shoulders. "Is that a yes to us?"

Yes, the goblin whispered.

I clasped my trembling hands behind my back. "It's a yes."

"Ah. And that makes you my what?" He cupped a hand to his ear.

"Property?" I patted my ass. "You want to brand me or something?"

"Porco Dio, only one person gets to bust my balls at every turn, so admit it or resign yourself to being nice to me forever after."

I smiled sweetly at him. "I'm your girlfriend."

"Wow. You got through the word without choking. Appreciate this beautiful Kodak moment."

"And I appreciate how you managed to sound grumpy and bastardy through that whole big speech of yours."

He smirked. "That worked for you, huh? Remember the sensitive side of me fondly, bella, because you won't be seeing it again. Good thing actually, I was starting to feel like one of Mitra's songs. The mushy one he wrote for Nava. Worse than his other emo bullshit." He slung an arm around me and led me back into the living room. "I will live my best grumpy, bastard, arrogant self."

"Who said anything about arrogant?"

He winked at me. "It's a package deal."

8

"How would you feel about me working this case with you? I know you're capable, but..." Drio punched the dining table. "I'm being used. And if there's one thing I can't stand, it's being jerked around."

As I knew well.

Even two months ago I might have refused him, but between Rabbi Mandelbaum's take-down and working on Ada, I'd had a lot of experience partnering with Rasha. Collaborating was pretty fun when it involved savvy individuals.

"You can help, but I'm in charge," I said.

"I respect that it's your case, but it's my life that was affected. I'm not taking a back seat."

"And I appreciate that, but you were compromised once and I don't know how susceptible you are to it happening again. If the demon is targeting you, I can both recognize and effectively deal with any further compulsions."

Ooh, that didn't sit well with hunter boy. Drio had no issues taking orders from a woman, he'd done it without hesitation with Nava and other witches, but it galled him to view himself as a liability.

"What if–" he began.

"Nope," I said cheerfully. "My case. My call. It's the smartest play here. Take it or leave it." *Take it.* I crossed my fingers that we would match wits and butt heads. "I won't shut you out."

He braced his elbows on his knees, his expression both serious and thoughtful. "I can't promise that if I think your well-being is at stake."

"You can have my back, but you can't take over because you want to protect me," I said. Kane and Ari had had the same fight. This wasn't about gender. "Remember, demons are part of my world as much as yours." I gave a wry smile. "More, actually."

He nodded reluctantly.

I pulled out the chair next to me and patted the seat.

"Grazie."

We spent an hour trolling through the demon dark web, but there were no mentions of Isabella's family, Drio, or anything about an enchanted ring.

Drio leaned back in his chair. "Demon boasting is worse than guys lying about sex."

"Almost as depraved, too." I clicked over to the part of Ada that housed what had formerly been the Brotherhood's database of demon knowledge. It had been expanded and revamped based on information we'd gotten from witches.

The profile I'd assembled yielded too many results of demon types at this point to be useful.

"Ada is impressive," Drio said. "Way better interface than the old database."

I kinda preened because the user interface had been my sweat and tears. There was a lot of psychology that went into crafting a user interface and it was great to be recognized by someone trained in that field.

We ran a search on magic artifacts that returned a number of records which we refined by the category of "ring." None of the results fit. Cursed diamonds had their own category, but even the smallest of those jewels were much larger than the one in this ring, and besides, they were all accounted for.

Drio examined the ring, twisting it around with a pencil to catch the light off its facets. He was smart enough not to touch it. "This didn't just fall into place, but I only decided to come talk to Antonia a couple of weeks ago. How did the demon know I'd be here? Or that Isabella would?"

"I don't know. Thoughts on the demon's agenda? Any recurring dreams or obsessive thoughts?"

"No. I've gone over everything. Marry Isabella. Go to Rome. There was nothing beyond that."

"If something does surface, Isabella is with her grandmother, so she should be safe," I said. "But the trade-off in breaking the compulsion was making the demon aware that it's been broken. It could come after you another way."

"I'm sure it will." He rubbed his hands in glee and a little thrill rushed through me.

I inspected both the iron bar and the ring. "The magic is still strong on both items. No marks or insignias on either piece. This is going to require a visit to the Appraiser."

"Who's that?"

"A brilliant half-demon," I said. "If she can't get us answers, no one can."

The Appraiser had set up shop in Antwerp, home of the diamond trade. There were no flights out tonight, but I booked us on one bright and early the next morning.

"This is good," I said. "It gives us time to procure her drugs."

"You didn't mention we needed to bring a gift." Drio's relaxed posture didn't change, but I shivered at the sudden temperature drop with his words.

"It's only polite. Plus, show up empty-handed and lose the hand."

"Tell me it's weed," he said.

I shook my head.

"Coke?"

Another shake.

"Meth."

I patted his cheek. "Aww. You sounded so hopeful there. No, it's Rust." A special tincture made out of two kinds of demon fluids, Rust wasn't sold to humans. It didn't have any effect on them, but demon dealers usually had enough other product to fuck people up, if not kill them outright. "If it makes you feel better, you can kill the dealer if she's targeting humans."

Drio brightened. "Why didn't you lead with that?"

"Because I am a thoughtful individual who enjoys giving the people she dates fun surprises." I tamped down on my grin. "Hey, do you have a safe? I'd like to lock these up."

We sealed the ring and the bar in a small Tupperware container. Cut down on the risk of accidentally touching them and keep them daisy fresh. Oh wait, that was douching.

Drio picked up the photo of the gondolier that no longer had glass. Clucking his tongue, he lay it on the table.

"Did you take these photos?" I said.

"Yeah. They're places where I had especially hard assignments. I took them to remind myself of the life and beauty there." Drio led me into a second bedroom that was set up as an office. Pushing aside the desk chair and rolling up the area rug, he lifted up a floorboard to reveal a small safe set into the ground.

If things went sideways with Drio, I was totally stealing his apartment because hidden safe in the floorboards? My childhood Nancy Drew self practically exploded in rapture.

His phone rang as he was opening the safe. "Ciao, Mom." He flinched, holding the phone away from his ear as his mother laid into him in a broad American accent. "I didn't! It wasn't–"

He shoved the phone at me. "Tell her I was compelled," he hissed.

"Coward," I said to him.

He nodded and shook the phone at me.

"Uh, hello? Mrs. Rossi?"

"Isabella, you poor dear." So weird that Drio had a mom who sounded like she was from the heartlands of America when he sounded like he was from the tenth level of Dante's Inferno. The sexy level where men with voices like sin and chocolate lived and did deliciously naughty things to deserving women and what was wrong with me, I was talking to his mother! I fished my mind out of the gutter.

"I'm not Isabella. My name is Leonie Hendricks, and I'm a private investigator hired to determine whether your son was compelled."

"Coward," Drio said.

I shot him the finger.

"Leonie Hendricks, shame on you. I saw the video. Are you or are you not my son's girlfriend?"

Swear to God, I was getting that damn video taken down. Also, why was everyone so label-happy? "Yes?"

"This isn't Jeopardy. You don't answer with a question."

I grit my teeth. "Yes, I'm his girlfriend."

Drio did a saucy little dance with some very interesting hip rolls, leaving me torn between wanting to stab him and rip his clothes off. Normal status quo.

"Why would you introduce yourself as a P.I.?" she said.

"I'm that, too."

"Technically, dear, you're an Associate. You're not Harry's full partner yet, though Drio says you'll end up with the business eventually and you definitely sound like you have the intelligence and drive to make anything happen."

I sat down heavily on the floor.

Drio locked up the safe, oblivious to my gobsmacked stare that he'd clearly discussed me with his mom. *Should I have spoken to my mother about him? Do I need to sit down and draw a timeline of how this relationship is supposed to progress?* Maybe with a color-coded Excel chart? Those were always good.

I gripped the phone, having missed her last few words. "Sorry?"

"I asked why you were being so formal? You're not some stranger."

I used my magic on myself in case *I* was under some compulsion because this was mind-bending, falling-down-a-rabbit-hole territory. I'd never spoken to Drio's mom in my life and she knew about my job, my boss, my title, and wanted us to be friends or something. "I'm not?"

"No. You say Drio was compelled?"

"Him and Isabella both. I'm working on tracking down why and what demon is behind it, though I may have to stop Antonia from cursing one or both of us at some point."

"That's very kind of you, dear. Put my son back on the phone, please."

"Okay. Nice speaking with you." I tossed Drio the phone like we were playing Hot Potato.

He laughed at me and walked out of the room.

I waited until his call was over, i.e. blatantly listened in, before seeking him out in his bedroom.

Drio was busy stripping the sheets off his bed. "Oh, that's the face of a woman who failed to learn anything incriminating while eavesdropping."

"Right? Stay put next time, Rossi. So, uh, you told your mom about us?"

He carried the bundle of sheets to his kitchen. "Haven't you?"

"Um."

"Am I your dirty secret?" The corners of his eyes crinkled in amusement as he stuffed the sheets into the small combo washer and dryer that sat in a small closet.

"Yeah. Along with the fact that I'm a half-demon, which she also doesn't know. News of their very existence had her doubling her nightly shot of bourbon."

"Ouch."

"It is what it is. Don't be offended that I haven't told her yet, okay? I love my mom, we just don't tend to talk about anything meaningful."

"My parents want us to come for dinner when all this is over." Drio added detergent. "Think you can handle that?"

"I ace parent interactions."

"Right."

I tsked him. "Sarcasm. We talked about this. Hey, why do you have a dryer? That's not typically Italian."

Drio shut the machine door. "Done some sleuthing into my people's habits to know me better?"

"Get over yourself, ego boy. My love affair with your country pre-dates any interactions with you."

"Mom's American and I grew up between here and the States. I like clothes that don't take three days to dry and fluffy towels, okay?" He adjusted the settings.

I rubbed his cheek. "Aw, little prince. Your delicate skin."

He scowled at me and swatted my hand away. "Yeah, well did you bring any normal clothes?"

I looked down at my sweater and pants. "How is this not normal?"

"It's not you. It's a disguise for the job. You're not wearing your bodyweight in jewelry, jingling like a cat with a bell every time you move, and that sweater isn't as touchable as your other stuff. Non mi piace." Drio hit the power button and the washer rumbled to life.

"Oh, well if his highness doesn't approve, I'll see what I can do." I secretly liked that he noticed I wasn't dressed like myself.

"Va bene." He flicked off the light to the laundry closet imperiously, master of his domain. Then he reached a hand back and patted the top of the washer twice, as if wishing it a bon voyage. I did the same thing in my building's laundry room and wondered if he'd named his machine, too. I almost laughed.

Instead, I wondered if two people with very definite opinions and a tendency to work alone could partner up and have it stick.

9

I made a few calls to find a Rust dealer here in Rome. Our chances would have been hit-and-miss anywhere else in Italy, but here in the largest city in the country, there was bound to be at least one demon pushing the drug.

"Got one." I came out of the office. "Drio?"

"Kitchen." Drio was bent over the open door of his fridge. I didn't see much beyond some wine, some beer, and a container of tomato sauce. The food situation was abysmal, but the view of his ass was a whole other story. One shelved firmly under "adults only."

"I got the name of a club where the local Rust dealer hangs out," I said.

He closed the fridge. "Where? Some dive around the train station?"

"It's called Limbo, in the Testaccio neighborhood."

"Are you sure? That's a trendy club."

"That's what my source said." I padded into the living room and pulled a wrinkled dress out of my messenger bag.

Drio peered inside. "How much stuff do you have crammed in there?"

"I am a master packer. Business casual and a good dress will get you through a lot of undercover work." I grabbed my travel make-up case and headed into his bathroom. "Where are your towels?"

He brought me a giant cream one, that yes, was very fluffy, stopping short when he saw the glass from the window laying on the bathroom floor and the scorch mark on the ceiling. "Isabella?"

Whoops. She'd missed a spot.

"The glass was me." Off his raised eyebrows, I said, "How do you think I got in, Mr. I-Have-An-Abloy-Protec2-Deadbolt? I had to pick your neighbor's lock, walk the ledge, and then break in here."

Drio crouched down, picked up the shards, and threw them in the trash. He raked a speculative gaze over me, his eyes so hot, I patted my legs to make sure my pants hadn't spontaneously combusted. "I don't suppose you'd consider getting naked right now, because fuck if your B&E isn't the sexiest thing I've heard in a long time."

"I am getting naked, but not with you. Work first." I pushed him toward the hallway.

"Does that mean play second?"

I batted my lashes at him. "Depends how good you are."

"Oh, bella. I'm very good."

"Yes, bello, but I'm better." With that, I shut the door on him.

I leaned back against it, enjoying a smug grin for a moment, then I turned the water on hot, hanging my dress up to steam the wrinkles out. After I'd showered, I dried my hair perfectly straight and gave myself a smoky look with green eyeliner that made my brown eyes pop. The rest of my make-up stayed fairly natural, including my lip gloss that was tinted the faintest apricot and plumped up my lips. I'd brought my favorite dress, a simple off-the-shoulder number in charcoal gray with three-quarter sleeves that was ruched along one hip. The dress fell to mid-calf and was quite elegant, until I walked and the thigh slit fell open. A pop of sexy.

For the final touch, I slid on the black heels I'd worn earlier. My foot was better but I was still happy for this rare pair of shoes that were both stylish and comfortable. Putting some sass in my stride, I flung open the bathroom door. This may have been a work night, but we were going to a trendy club and I looked fantastic. Let the sexual tension commence.

I was greeted with a wolf whistle. I did a little turn for his perusal and then nearly swallowed my tongue.

Drio stood with his hands loosely tucked into the pockets of his dark gray pants that flowed over his hard thighs like water. His open jacket was the same color. His white shirt had the top two buttons open, a light dusting of blond hair peeking through. The sleeves were rolled up to his mid-forearm, exposing ropy muscle, and if that wasn't enough to make me press my legs tight together, over the shirt, Drio wore a light grey button-up vest with the bottom button undone.

And glasses. Dear God, he wore glasses. His blond hair was artfully disheveled above the heavy black frames.

"Glasses. That's not… I didn't know… Glasses."

He pushed them up his nose. "Yeah. I got them when I came home last time. Wear them at night for driving."

"It's good to be safe." Did we have time for me to rip his clothes off, lick him all over, and put him back together again?

"Probably not if you want to get to that dealer."

I groaned. "I said that out loud."

"With special enunciation on the 'all over,'" he said helpfully.

My cheeks almost combusted, I blushed so badly.

"If it's any consolation, I'm so hard looking at you right now that I can't think straight. Several of the things I want to do to you may be illegal and all are definitely immoral." He dropped a kiss on my head.

"That makes it better." I grabbed the tiny clutch that was

also in my messenger bag–yes, I really was a phenomenal packer–and held out my hand. "Ready?"

He stared at it a moment, then a dazzling smile lit up his face and he folded his fingers over mine, engulfing them in his warmth and strength. "So ready."

We strolled through his neighborhood, Drio all loose-limbed, keeping tight hold of my hand as he pointed out local businesses and characters. Since we had time to kill before the club opened, he'd insisted on treating me to dinner so I didn't injure him from lack of food.

We stopped in front of a small bistro where a crowd of people stood outside chatting. The air was as thick with laughter as it was with cigarette smoke.

Drio frowned, tapping his toes. Then he abruptly pointed at the restaurant. "Do you want to try my favorite trattoria? It's not fancy, but the risotto with radicchio and speck is incredible."

So, this was a regular hang-out of his? Did he bring a lot of dates here?

"Never mind." He tugged on my arm. "We'll go somewhere else."

"No. I want to try this place." The aroma wafting out made my stomach grumble.

He looked relieved… and the tiniest bit apprehensive? "Good."

Several of the people greeted Drio while I received more than one curious look. Drio deflected the more pointed questions in good-natured Italian.

The restaurant was clean and airy with light wood beams on the ceilings and white brick walls. A leather banquette ran the length of the back and the packed cozy tables left little room to navigate, but servers glided around the organized chaos with a fluid ease.

A bald man in a baggy suit, who I presumed was the owner, raised a hand at Drio. He did a double take when he saw me, then his face creased in a sly grin.

Drio tensed and scowled at him.

The man hurried over to speak to me in Italian, but I could only pick up a handful of words.

Drio cut him off. "English, Vito. This is Leonie."

"Ciao, bellissima. Welcome." Vito grabbed a couple of menus.

"Grazie," I said.

He hustled aside an older couple to lead us to a table, but this was Italy and they weren't going to take that quietly. A furious argument ensued, complete with a lot of vaguely threatening hand gestures. Especially from the woman.

"Oh!" Drio yelled back at them with a few choice words. Then Vito yelled a few more things.

I tugged on Drio's sleeve. "Let them go first."

"What?" The woman who had been arguing with Vito shooed me to the table. "No. You go. Sit. Please. Enjoy your dinner. Drio never brings anyone here. Right, Carmella?"

"Che vuoi?" A buxomy blonde looked up from behind the bar, managing to perfectly fill three wine glasses without spilling a drop. She looked between Drio and me and broke out in a cackling laugh before making the sound of a whip.

He sighed.

I ducked my head into Drio's sleeve.

He leaned down so his mouth brushed my ear. "You're blushing again."

"Because I have no idea what's going on, whether I should laugh at all the jokes with everyone else or if I should be mortified."

"Oh no, the one who should be mortified is definitely me," he said.

"Basta! Leave the poor girl alone. Go, bella. Enjoy." The older woman bestowed a kind smile on me. "We like to tease this one." She angled her head at Drio.

"No shit," he muttered.

We followed Vito to the table where he handed us our menus. Drio ordered two glasses of wine and Vito snorted.

"Big shot is trying to impress you. You'll drink the house wine. I made it. Tastes better."

"Sounds good," I agreed.

Vito nodded sagely. "Bene. You brought a smart girl. Davide owes me five euro." Whistling, he hustled off.

"Davide bet I'd bring someone brainless?" Drio made an obscene arm gesture at a male server striding past with a full tray.

The server smirked at him, patting him on the head.

"You usually eat alone?" I said.

Drio shrugged. "Half the time I end up sitting with one of this crowd, but if the question is do I bring dates here? I don't date."

I bit my lip. "You have Rohan and your other Rasha friends. Don't you come here with them?"

"I have friends all over the world and I've had great times with them, but this is one of those places I keep for myself."

But he was sharing it with me. I dropped my gaze to my menu which was in Italian. Thanks to my French, I only had to ask Drio a few clarifying questions.

"You studied in French with Nava and Ari," he said.

"Yup. Very handy for having conversations we didn't want our parents to understand."

"You three must have been terrors together."

"Ari tried to stay out of our craziness, but he was always there to come pick us up. Bail us out."

"Do I want to know?" he said.

"About which time?"

"A woman with a record." Drio fanned himself.

Vito returned with a small decanter and two glasses. He poured me some and checked that I liked it before taking our orders.

88

"Insalata mista, tomato bruschetta, grilled calamari, and crab and lobster ravioli," I said.

"This is to share?" Vito said.

I clutched my menu possessively. "No."

Vito kissed his fingers. "A woman who eats. Leonie, you are always welcome here."

"Va fangul, Vito." Drio poured wine into his glass since Vito hadn't bothered. "You gonna take my order?"

"Why? Is it different from the last sixty times you were here? You want risotto and then the vitello al marsala. He's very boring," Vito said to me. "Me, I like different experiences."

"That's why I expect your food will be divine." I handed him my menu.

He took Drio's as well, and then swatted him on top of his head with them. "Took you long enough to find this one."

There was a call from the kitchen and Vito scurried off.

"Vito's not going to let me in if I don't bring you with me next time." Drio's eyes sparkled behind his frames, but there was a wariness in how he held himself.

I raised my glass. "Then here's to many more visits."

Drio relaxed, an infectious smile lighting up his face as he clinked his glass to mine. "I'll drink to that."

10

The rest of dinner passed in a haze of good food and good conversation. I practically rolled out the door afterward, I was so full. But first, I had to bid each of the staff and some of the customers a heartfelt ciao, because we were now on a first name basis.

I stretched up and kissed Drio. "Thank you. That was wonderful."

Dates were good. Sweet, slow ways of getting to know each other. I hadn't had a lot of those because there weren't that many people I'd been interested in getting to know.

Drio tucked my hand into the crook of his elbow and led me through the labyrinthine streets. Neither of us filled the silence with small talk, content to people watch and soak in the night. He stopped in front of a sleek, silvery-blue, vintage convertible with chrome detailing and unlocked my door. She was the exact same color as my Vespa. Great minds.

Since it was October, the soft top was on the car.

"Meet the Goddess," he said.

"You and Ro and your car names." I bounced on the black leather seat, testing it for comfort-level. Very nice.

Drio slid in on the driver's side. "It's a 1965 Citroën DS."

"Ah. Déesse. Like 'goddess' in French. Cute."

Drio started the engine, his biceps flexing as he pulled out of the tight parking spot.

We made our way through Rome past charming apartment buildings and busy streets pulsing with nightlife. Church spires peeked up coyly from side streets and stone faces on old walls gushed water into basins. I'd teased him in the past about driving like a nonna, but I was kind of disappointed at how boring his vehicular handling actually was.

Drio wove past a weird stone pyramid in front of an ancient Roman wall, pointing out Porta San Paolo, the castle-like building next to it.

This was the most relaxed we'd ever been together. If our entire relationship could be like this, I could handle it. Once this situation with the compulsion was dealt with, I was all for building more moments and memories like this one.

However, I didn't forget the real reason I was here. That dark agenda lurked in every slithered shadow, every gust of wind that spiked the chilled night air, right until we arrived at the nightclub.

Drio parked at the valet stop.

From the outside, Limbo didn't look like much. There was a discreet door behind a well-muscled bouncer, who was menacing any of the well-dressed patrons in line behind the velvet rope who tried to get in before they were deemed worthy.

"How long do you think we have to wait?" I said. There were at least twenty people ahead of us, and it was only 10PM.

"Fuck waiting." Drio got out of the Citroën, tossing his keys to the female valet in the smart black outfit, and strode up to the bouncer. Pure hunter, he wore his ineffable confidence with a casualness the way most people wore a comfortable sweater. He was top tier on the food chain, which was annoying because it was true.

It didn't mean the bouncer needed to pump up Drio's already enormous ego by practically presenting his neck to his new alpha.

Drio spoke no more than three words to him before the guy stepped aside to usher us in, latching the rope behind me to the dismay of the grumbling crowd.

A dimly-lit foyer led to clubs on three different levels: one upstairs that had posters for a live band, one on the ground floor that was pumping out jazz electronica, and a windy staircase leading to the basement.

Basement it was.

The club on the lower level wasn't so much a feast for the senses as a dodgy buffet with pretensions above its station. The red carpeting featured a repeating pattern of the evil eye: a single eyeball outlined in black. Not only was the carpet wall-to-wall, it was wall-to-ceiling. Red velvet sofas ran the length of the room and in case we still didn't get the theme, the space was bathed in red spotlights.

Skinny fashionistas were draped over the furniture like bored cats.

On the far wall an abstract metal skeleton, easily six feet tall, was chained to the only patch of wall not carpeted.

I nudged Drio. "You think that was the designer?"

He eyed the sculpture. "Should'a left him alive to relive this hell every single night."

"Not sure he would have survived the ennui in here." I fanned the air. "The disaffected malaise is thick enough to choke a horse."

Drio guffawed and crossed his arms. The simple motion of his biceps flexing rippled out through the club, drawing every eye our way. Drio glowered at them until most of the people turned away like that had been their intention all along.

"Subtle," I said. "And precisely why I'm going to find the dealer on my own."

"I can tone it down."

I laughed.

He dropped his arms and tried to assume a meek expression. "I'm very good at getting answers."

"So am I. You are a blunt hammer. We're in a crowded nightclub. The situation calls for precision and finesse."

Drio looked around. "Did you outsource?"

"Ha. Ha. Leash your inner control freak and back me up from a distance."

"Inner control *tendencies*. Full-fledged freak was never an official diagnosis."

"Look, the demon is going to recognize you as Rasha and I'd rather not have to chase it in heels once it does. I'm just a cute unthreatening female." I propped a hip against a couch then flinched away because it had this bonkers texture that was sucking my dress into it. "Are you angry?"

He exhaled, arms still crossed, and shadows played around his cheekbones. "No. You clearly know what you're doing and you're right. You can get the jump on the demon in a way that I can't. I have your back and if there's trouble, I'll be there." He frowned as if something had just occurred to him, then shook his head and stepped aside to let me pass.

"Something's clearly still troubling you."

"Not you. I promise." He kissed my cheek. "Keep your head in the game and if you need me, signal in some way."

"I'll put my hair behind my ear."

"Got it. Good luck." He melted into the crowd at the large main bar.

I blinked. In a matter of seconds, I'd lost sight of him. He was a tall man, taller than a lot of the people in here, yet it took me a solid minute to find him again. He leaned on the bar ordering a drink. Someone jostled my elbow, and I automatically turned to see who it was. By the time I glanced back at Drio, he was gone again.

This wasn't his flash-stepping magic. It was more the way a

big cat hides in the tall grass with infinite patience, all but invisible to its prey.

The thought of his green eyes gleaming in the dim light while focused on me made my nipples go hard, but I didn't feel like prey. Quite the opposite. I had a primal tug to hunt him back, see who could establish dominance. The whole "here, wolfie," thing but without the running away part.

I gazed into a darkened corner, my gaze meeting his dead on. A coy smile curled my lips.

He narrowed his eyes, but I ducked around a group of women who'd just entered, momentarily blocking myself from his view.

After a quick scan of the room, I opted for the smaller bar in the back corner which allowed me to cross the room and observe the clientele. When I didn't know what my target looked like, my approach was two-fold. First, I did a broad sweep of the environment. The point was not to focus on anything, but rather see if anything twigged my internal alarm. If nothing did, I examined the space more thoroughly, making a short-list of people who fit my criteria. For a dealer, that might be someone who preferred to stay in a corner keeping a low profile and letting a stream of people come to them, or alternately, it might be someone who left the room a lot.

That might narrow it down to one potential candidate, but if there was more than one, I checked for glamours. Full demons who interacted with people required a human form. But glamours often had tells. A shimmering of air like heat rippling off hot concrete, especially around the throat. Also, a lot of demons were sloppy with their glamours, resulting in ears that were a bit too pointy, or teeth that were slightly too canine.

It could be tougher to determine half-demons, because not all of us had a demon form to revert to. Our human form was our one and only body, no glamour required. Generally, between all of my checks, I found my target a solid ninety-percent of the time.

I ordered a glass of wine and did my broad sweep. My gaze snagged on a beautiful woman with a glossy pixie cut and a slightly tomboyish build. She wore a slinky black pantsuit with a halter top that showed off her toned arms. A cool chunky gold bracelet curved around her left bicep.

The woman reminded me of my good friend and former hook-up Madison.

I glided over to the table that she occupied by herself. "Mind if I join you?"

She looked up from her phone with a rueful smile. "Mi dispiace, ma non parlo inglese."

"Parlez-vous français?"

"Ah, oui. Asseyez-vous." She gestured to the stool next to her. "Je m'appelle Giulia."

"Léonie. Enchantée." I gave her my hand and she held it for a moment longer than necessary.

It was all signals go.

We were two attractive young women with a healthy appreciation of the other in a nightclub that, ridiculous décor aside, was pumping out a bluesy groove that was sex with a horn section. By the time I'd finished my wine, we'd escalated to light touches.

I loved women's bodies: the softness of their skin, the curves and swells. Being with guys like Drio was like wearing my favorite leather jacket, rugged, sleek, and all of it cloaked in a dark edge. Touching Giulia was like working with my favorite yarn, a velvet glide that slipped through my fingers, sweetly pliant. Both appealed to me for different reasons, and I wasn't a traitor or a fake if I liked one better.

My fingers traced lazy circles on her toned skin, wistful. I wished more people got it, or at least tried to understand. But then Giulia was telling me in a sultry voice about the DJ who played upstairs Friday nights, how she'd danced until she'd broken a heel, and the way her eyes scrunched up when she smiled made me forget about all the bad things in the world for a moment.

She opened her handbag to apply a fresh swipe of lipstick and the faintest scent of apples floated out. I glanced into her clutch which was filled with tiny sealed baggies filled with white powder. Oh, I knew what this was. This stuff was nasty. People snorted it, thinking it was coke, but it wasn't. It was a demon secretion that induced a violent rage in the user.

I asked her if she had a cigarette to share.

She picked up her purse and held out her hand. I took it, letting her lead me through a fire exit door that had been propped open to allow the cool air in and the smokers out.

It led to a tiny courtyard that we had to ourselves. I shivered and Giulia ran her hands up and down my arms.

"Cold?" she purred, still speaking French.

I pressed her up against the wall and nipped at her earlobe, inhaling her floral perfume, and savoring the feel of her skin under my hands. Would this be the last time I'd ever get to be with a girl? Another reason to take things slowly with Drio. I had never chosen to be exclusive with either gender, never mind with a single person. It was a big deal. I had no regrets about wanting to be with him, but it was still an adjustment.

I lowered my lashes, coyly. "You could warm me."

Skimming my hands down along the sides of her halter top, I plucked the vial of Rust from her bra and palmed it. I wobbled as if I'd snagged a heel.

"Whoops." I giggled and bent down to adjust my shoe. Then I grabbed Giulia's ankle and squeezed, sending my magic into it. She disappeared, dead.

Her clutch with the drugs fell to the ground.

She was a demon and she preyed on people and while I couldn't leave her alive, I mourned her loss. Giulia had been beautiful and vivacious, and for a moment under these low lights, we'd simply been two women enjoying each other's company. I'd destroyed that, though I'd never regret adhering to my moral code. Sometimes that choice was easy, or well, easier, like with the asper. Other times, it came with a sliver of grief that became part of my soul. I had chosen a far different path than Giulia, but to many people in this world, we were both monsters.

At least, I'd gotten the Rust. I tossed the vial in the air triumphantly. Someone behind me snatched it before I could catch it again.

Drio. My body had relaxed against his before I consciously registered it was him.

He wrapped an arm around me. "I wasn't sure if I was being ditched or set up for a threesome." His voice vibrated against my back.

"You catch more flies with honey." I twisted around in his hold. "Would you? A threesome?"

"Is it my birthday?"

"Yeah, yeah, two chicks. Every guy's fantasy." I took the Rust from him and put it in my bra to keep it warm against my skin.

His eyes tracked my movement. "Not that it would be a hardship, but you're attracted to women. Why should you give that up? It also doesn't have to be two women." My mouth fell open and Drio laughed. "I've hooked up with a few guys," he said. "Not Rasha. That's a hard no for me."

"I can work with that."

His eyes glinted wickedly behind his glasses, and he ran a hand along the thigh slit in my dress.

"Sorry, you didn't get to kill her," I said.

He stilled, then shrugged. "Probably better this way. How did you know she was the dealer?"

"I suspected because of the gold cuff. Auger demon."

"Clever. Distinctive patchy skin on her left bicep." He slid his hands around to cup my ass over the dress.

"Jewelry is a fairly common way to hide it, plus they always use gold." I arched against his erection. "The patchiness is a bacteria that lives on their skin."

"While the gold dims the glow the bacteria emit." He rushed his words in his excitement at our shared knowledge, but his hips pressed into me in time in a slow roll, in time with the new jam sliding along my skin like a sinuous siren's song. "Deconstructing demon tells with you may be my new kink. Most guys just want to bag and tag. This talk's too nerdy for them. I like this."

"Me too." Drio had a degree in psychology and I was doing mine in criminology. There was so much we could riff off together. I ran my hands over his olive skin, his muscled torso taking second place to his brain in how intoxicating I found him. "Unraveling mysteries is the shit," I said. "I'm really lucky Harry gave me the opportunity to do this."

"Did he give you 'the opportunity' to break and enter?" Yeah, he did the finger quotes.

I laughed. "Oh yeah. He kept changing the locks on the office door on payday. He'd stand inside in the front window cackling and holding up my check."

"Sounds fun."

"It was, but he's lost his taste for much of this over the past year." I pushed the sadness away that if Harry retired, I'd be doing this by myself with only his creepy kitten paintings to keep me company, and curled my leg around Drio's thigh. "Wanna know how I confirmed my suspicions about the demon?"

Drio mock-shivered. "Tell me, baby."

I whispered against his ear. "She enabled Night Shift mode on her phone."

"Because augers are light sensitive."

Okay, Drio might actually know more about demons than I did. I almost came right then and there. I fucking loved it.

"Gold star for you." I moved his hand between my legs.

"No, pretty sure you're winning all gold stars making that demon." Drio groaned into my hair. "You're not wearing underwear."

I spread my legs wider. "How many gold stars do I get for that?"

He slid his finger inside me and my head fell back against the brick wall.

"How'd you find the vial?" His voice was husky, his finger sliding over my wet heat.

"Rust needs to be kept warm. The obvious place was against her skin, plus I saw the outline of the vial stuffed into the side of her bra when she raised her arm." My voice hitched.

"You didn't need my help at all."

"Is that a bad thing?"

He crushed his lips to mine. His kiss devoured me, his talented fingers reducing me to a shaky, moaning mess.

My body went up in flames. I hung on to his belt loops and let myself be consumed.

"The total fucking opposite of a bad thing," he growled.

His finger flitted once more over my clit and I came hard, shuddering in his arms.

"Home. Now," he said.

I stuttered out a laugh. "You just finger-fucked me in a courtyard. I need a moment. New rule. You need to be the strong-willed one and make sure this doesn't happen again."

"Yeah, no. Not gonna happen." He surveyed the courtyard and club entrance. "No one saw us. You're good."

Good? No, I was freaking fabulous. Picking up Giulia's clutch, I swayed, sex-drunk, out of the club, touching my fingers to my swollen lips.

The valet brought Drio's car around.

I clicked my seat belt in, grateful to be tethered down. Tonight had undone me. Drio didn't just value my independence and my particular skill sets, he got off on them. Plus, he was bisexual? I pinched myself. He was an android, someone specially designed for me, that was the only possibility. I laughed, filled with such a lightness that if I wasn't strapped in, I swore I'd float out into the night, hovering like a balloon over the pulsing city.

Drio's teeth flashed in the streetlights, and his fingers curled around the gear shift like a pianist before a concert. I could get used to this, the breathless nights and unexpected sweetness.

Until he pulled into traffic and everything shattered.

11

Drivers in Rome were a terrifying bunch. Drio, now apparently focused on getting back to his place with a single-minded determination that was fairly glorious when I wasn't clutching my seat convinced that I would die, left them in the dust. I swear his flash-step magic extended to his car because that was the only way he jammed us into some of those slivers he called "openings" in other lanes. By the time he'd wedged us into something approximating a parking spot, I was breathing heavily and not from arousal.

I unclawed my fingers from the grooves I'd worn into the side of my seat.

Drio peeled himself out of the car. "You're looking a little tense."

"You think?"

He flash-stepped us from the car to the building's hallway, then up the stairs, to his floor, and into his room. It took six heartbeats.

Once inside, he got a heating pad to wrap the Rust in so it would stay warm. He draped his blazer over a chair, a dark silhouette without the lights on, then unbuttoned his vest and tossed that aside as well. He moved like a work of art. Michelangelo's statues were shlubby hack jobs of the male form in comparison.

I kicked off my heels–one wobbled and fell over–and held out my hand. "Take me to–" I dropped my hand and looked around the apartment, realizing what I'd failed to notice during my break-in. "Wait. You don't have wards."

"That conversation started properly."

"You always stayed at the Brotherhood chapter house in Vancouver, and I couldn't be with you there because of the wards. That's why I made excuses to bring you home with me. There aren't any here on your apartment, but there were. You mentioned it before. Did you take them down for me?"

"It's not a big deal. I can protect myself."

I pushed him onto the sofa and straddled him. "I know. I like that about you."

"I like that about you, too. Though life would be easier with a damsel in distress who'd let me take care of everything." His blond brows were dark slashes while his cheekbones gave him a ruggedness that his full lips undermined. Those decadent lips. He raked his gaze over me, his lashes sweeping his cheek and rendering his green eyes to emerald slits.

"Not half as much fun though," I said. "You'd have to climb all those locked towers and wash off dragon stink and there's less time for things like ripping your clothes off, licking you all over, and putting you back together again."

He nodded, serious. "Right. Damsels are highly overrated."

I took off his glasses and placed them on the small table next to the sofa, then tugged his white shirt free and popped open the buttons, exposing his gorgeous olive skin that I skimmed my fingers over. I gave a breathy kind of purr that made his dick twitch in response and made me want to preen like a cat. The coarse wool of his pants bit into my flesh, a carnal edge heightening my pleasure, and I rubbed myself against him.

Drio reached for me, but I placed his hands on the top of the sofa.

"No touching me yet."

He dug his fingers into the leather, his cheeks flushed and a fierce expression on his face.

I leaned back, surveying him, filled with a giddy rush. This predator who scared the monsters in the shadows, who could destroy me, held himself in check at my command. This was our first time together in months and I wanted to savor the anticipation of it for a moment, though a frisson of fear snaked through me. Ever since I'd come to Rome, my goblin had been awakened in unexpected ways. To have her come out in the middle of sex would be a disaster. Fully letting go with Drio was a nice wish, but I didn't dare.

There was desire in his gaze, but there was also that hunter's watchfulness assessing me, so I threw him a cheeky grin and sucked his nipple into my mouth. I was rewarded with an incoherent moan. Licking, sucking, biting, I explored his chest, raking my nails along his six-pack. I trailed my lips down his torso and along the soft dusting of hair leading into his pants, catching every ridge.

He smelled of soap and tasted the tiniest bit of salt. His abs rippled under my tongue, dragged over his muscles in exquisite slowness.

Drio watched me with hot eyes, and through my edgy haze, I grew wet.

"I want to go down on you." I circled the button of his pants with my finger. "All the times we had sex, you never let me."

"I haven't let anyone. Not in a very long time."

"Why?"

He pressed his lips together, then gave a tiny head shake, as if admitting the answer for the first time. "Same reason I didn't kiss. That kind of intimacy means something. The position forces me to look at them and it makes it real on another level."

"You have to look at the person you're with during sex."

He shrugged. "Not the way I did it."

But he'd looked at me when we'd had sex. Every time. No

matter what position we started in, it had always ended with him stretched out over me, his emerald eyes burning into mine.

The same way they burned into me now. I pressed a hand against my stomach, feeling my ragged inhale. Drio and I had started out as chemistry and game-playing. A dangerous secret that we hid from our friends. That he had issues was obvious, but even when my feelings for him had changed into something deeper, I hadn't probed.

What would have happened if I'd asked him why he didn't kiss? Would he have told me about his past? Could we have somehow navigated the slippery feelings of hurt and betrayal on both sides?

My eyes intent on his, I popped the button of his pants open and drew down the zipper, the sound shocking in the silence. His cock strained against his underwear, some tight number that probably cost a fortune in a pricey men's boutique.

His fingers tightened on the leather, but he didn't stop me.

Sliding off him, I dropped a cushion onto the floor and kneeled on it to wriggle his pants and underwear down. I admired his thick, hard length, flicking my tongue against the head.

Drio hissed. He watched me with a preternatural stillness, the eye of the hurricane, wanting to release the full force of his passion, but chaining himself down to please me.

I licked his shaft like he was a Tootsie Pop that I needed to get to the center of.

"Tease," he growled.

For that, I wrapped my lips around his cock, taking almost all of him in one long, slow slide.

He arched his hips with a sigh, positioning my hand around the base of his dick. He just kept lowering his guard, putting himself utterly in my hands, allowing himself to be at my mercy. It was a gift that I didn't take lightly.

My hair fell forward in a red curtain around me. I squeezed

his cock, running my hand up and down his erection as I sucked him off.

Drio pulled my hair aside. "I need to see you."

He did. More than anyone.

I dug my fingers into his hips, tugging him toward me, forcing him deeper. Drio sped up his thrusts, his movements rougher, wilder, and I reached down to play with myself. My body throbbed. I couldn't take him in fast enough to slake my all-consuming craving for him.

Drio leaned forward, grabbed my wrist and sucked my fingers into his mouth. "Vieni qui, bella. Vieni a prendermi."

Come here, beautiful. Come and get me. Damn, if I didn't moan and rock forward.

I rose up off my knees, my shoulder blade catching the corner of the coffee table, and kissed Drio with everything I had, everything I could give him.

Drio swallowed my gasp of pain with his mouth, his hand coming around to soothe the spot. He pulled me astride him once more, trailing kisses down my neck, his lips skating over the hollow of my throat. All he wore was his shirt, mostly falling off his shoulders by now, while I still had my dress on.

I rocked against his silky hardness and threaded my fingers into his hair.

That was as far as I got before he flipped us over and his mouth crashed down on mine. Need slammed into me like a fist.

Drio rose onto his knees and I reached for him, desperate for the press of his body back. He grasped the sides of my dress and in one swift motion, pulled it over my head, letting it flutter to the floor. Under his clever, impatient hands, my bra fluttered free. He sucked my breast into his mouth, his teeth rasping over my tight nipple. The lust-soaked need in Drio's eyes made me shiver and want to stoke him higher.

I grabbed his open shirtfront and dragged his mouth back to mine, slamming our bodies together. The kiss grew rough and messy, his mouth hot, almost punishing. Heat blazed through my body like a fireball.

"Ho voglia di scoparti," he said huskily.

"What?"

He thrust against me.

"Oh. Yes. Get a condom."

"Sì." Drio looked mind-whacked, his eyes glazed over and blown out. He fumbled on the floor for his pants, pulling a condom out and sliding it over the tip of his cock, before placing my hand over top. "Put it on me. Feel what you do to me."

He was velvet over steel.

We fell back against the sofa, Drio rocking against me without entering.

"Why are you holding back?" I said.

"Because you are. I feel it, bella."

"I'm…" My lie tasted like ash.

He was right. I had been holding back, and it hadn't mattered because my goblin woke up anyway. Curiosity emanated off her like she was sussing Drio out. She hummed in recognition, craving his darkness, and for the first time in my life, we were in perfect agreement. I swallowed, my throat dry. I wasn't ready to cede control of my demon, give her free rein, but after everything that had played out tonight, I wanted Drio at his wildest and I'd go as far as I could.

My iron-clad control relaxed and a fierce breathlessness tore through me. I ripped up every plan I'd had for taking it slow and smart. That wasn't us. We were volcanic and quicksilver clever.

Despite the hurt, after everything that had happened today, I was choosing to trust in him.

Choosing to trust in us.

I kissed him, long, slow, and honey sweet.

Drio pulled back to regard me steadily. Then he nodded, understanding my answer. My commitment. He brushed a strand of hair out of my face. "That's what I'm talking about."

"Are you going to fuck me now?" I said. Ew. That sounded so needy. "Fuck me."

He ignored me, sucking on my other tit. With one hand he pinned my hands above my head, continuing to slide against me and play with my clit.

Every encounter with my redcap had been a battle of snarling and hissing and quelling her rage at being shackled. Yet, Drio had taken control here and she was rolling over and exposing her belly, purring in satisfaction.

She wasn't wrong.

I arched up under his touch, electricity thrumming through my nerve endings, my entire body an inferno, and dissolved into staccato and heat.

The leather squeaked underneath me, and I clung to his shoulders, rubbing myself against him, faster and faster, until the wild spiral whipping inside me peaked, and I came hard.

"*Now* I'll fuck you," he whispered and thrust so deeply inside me, I cried out.

He immediately stopped, his eyes intent on mine. His grip loosened, his touch gentle where it had been bruising. Drio the hunter could kill me; Drio the man would never hurt me. Not anymore.

"Move," I growled, digging my nails into his ass.

He ravished my mouth, his tongue meeting mine with abandon as he drove into me with savage thrusts.

"Cosi mi piaci. Sono tutta tuo." His fucking was as merciless as his murmured Italian was seductive.

New flames of pleasures rippled through me, stoking higher and hotter. He was inside me and around me and under my skin. I shut my eyes, lost to an intimacy so profound my entire world jolted sideways, rearranged under the staggering realization that this was the person who might make me believe in "The One."

I screamed, shuddering under him, my next orgasm hitting me hard enough to momentarily blind me.

Drio came right after, biting my shoulder lightly. He stayed stretched out over me, burying his head in the crook of my neck.

The room stank of musk, the only sound our relaxed breathing.

My goblin was content. No fighting, and for once, no rage. Just an unexpected, yet extremely relaxed bliss. Was there another way forward for her and me? Drio had unlocked this glimmer of possibility, but she and I had been combatants for so long, I didn't know what a truce would mean. What it would look like. Who I'd become.

What I'd become.

"Do I have to give you another orgasm and get you out of your head?" he said.

"You think you could?"

He gave me a smug smile.

"Ruthless move unleashing the Italian dirty talk on me, Rossi."

Drio ducked his head. "I was having trouble remembering my English."

I ran my foot along his calf. "I'm not sure if I should be insulted that our previous hook-ups didn't decimate your bilingualism or just be flattered."

He chuckled. "Flattered."

"It was different tonight." I played with his hair. He'd sweated out the product that had been in it, the strands smooth and pale in the moonlight filtering through the curtains.

"Because you stopped holding back."

"It wasn't just me. Was it?"

He rolled onto his side to face me. "Tonight, us, was everything that I've wanted for years. No one's ever shared every part of my life with me. Not like you do. So yeah, it had to be different."

"Mon petit ami." I kissed him.

He dazzled me with an unguarded smile that made champagne bubbles erupt inside me. *Mine.*

"I officially get boyfriend status?" he said. "You can't take it back, you know."

"I don't want to."

A shy smile stole across his face, then he blushed and slid a pillow over his head.

My heart melted at this vulnerable side of him. Ever since Nava and Rohan had gotten together, she'd walked around with this look like she had a secret. Now I had one, too. Getting to be the one person in the world that saw this amazing man undone and laid bare, body and soul. I permitted myself a smug smile of my own. While he couldn't see it, of course.

The smile stayed on my face throughout my shower. I hummed as I lathered up, thinking about my boyfriend.

Mate, my goblin pronounced.

I squeezed the soap so hard that it flew from my hand and pinged off the shower wall. It was one thing to be cool with calling Drio my boyfriend, to acknowledge that he might make me *believe* in "The One," and quite another to have the deepest, most primal part of myself declare him "my forever and ever person" according to goblin culture.

I picked up the soap with trembling hands, my blood running cold despite the heat of the spray. There was an exceedingly specific ritual involved in formalizing a pair-bond between goblins and even if one day in the very far future we were at that point, there was no way I could ask Drio to participate. It was too freakish. But if she had made up her mind, would I have any say otherwise? I pushed it very far down the list of things to deal with.

After I'd showered and towel dried my hair best I could, I wrapped myself in Drio's cotton robe that came down to my ankles, rolling up the sleeves so I didn't look like a child.

Drio had gone to take his shower and I had business to attend to.

The heating pad was on low and the Rust tincture was its normal light green. I left it where it was and retrieved Giulia's purse, spreading the small bags of drugs she'd had on the kitchen counter.

I found a metal mixing bowl and added about a cup of vinegar to the bowl. Then I snipped the corners of the packets open and shook the powder into the pungent liquid, careful not to spill any or send up a cloud of dust.

"What are you doing?" Drio wandered in wearing a pair of boxer shorts, his hair damp. He pressed a kiss to my shoulder, smelling like sandalwood soap.

My goblin hummed in satisfaction.

My stomach twisted, but I mustered up a smile. "There's only one way to dispose of this stuff safely. If I flush it or wash it down the drain, I risk contaminating the water supply. I have to detox it first."

"You can do that to substances and not just people? Cool."

"It is, rather." I tossed the plastic bags out in the trash, the corners of my lips dancing in a smile.

"Why the vinegar?" He peered over my shoulder, running his hand along my spine in slow strokes.

I swirled the powder and liquid together. "It's easier to detoxify something if it's in liquid form. See, detoxification is the most important aspect to goblin magic. They consume blood and they need a way to purify it since goblins don't discriminate between human, animal, and other demons."

"It's a food source," Drio said. "It needs to be free of contaminants and blood could carry disease or toxins."

"Exactly." I plunged my hand into the bowl and released my magic. A bluish-white goo spread up from the mixture over my fingertips, coating me up to my wrists.

"How do you know when it's clean?"

"I can feel the purity level. That should do it. You can dump it out now."

Drio rinsed the leftover mixture down the drain. "What about what's on your skin?"

"It's harmless. It just looks gross." I washed my hands thoroughly. "Ta da."

Drio handed me a dish towel to dry my hands. "You hungry?"

"Assume the answer is always yes."

"Right. You need to metabolize energy on a regular basis. You're on chopping duty." Drio got me a cutting board, knife and a large head of garlic. "We need eight cloves."

"Eight? Good thing we already had sex."

He prepped the water and set it to boil, then grated some parmesan and cut up lemons. While the entire package of linguine was cooking, he heated up some chili oil in a pan and added the lemons, kosher salt, and a splash of wine. "Garlic, please."

I dumped my chopped-up mound, inhaling deeply at the yummy sizzle of melding flavors. "Do you eat this a lot?"

"Yeah. It's one of the only things I can make, and it's good, late-night food. I used to make it for the guys here in Rome after a hunt." Drio grabbed a wooden spoon and tossed the ingredients together.

"Where is the rest of your chapter?" I said.

"Some are here. Some teamed up with Mandelbaum, and I don't know or care what happened to them. They were assholes and I hope they got what was coming. My buddy Marco was one of the people who lost their magic to Gog and Magog."

"How's he doing?"

Drio blinked away his sad expression. "Dealing."

"About that." I took the wooden spoon from him and stirred the sauce. "When you stopped me from touching them, you didn't just save my magic. You saved my life."

He put his hand over mine, stopping the stirring. "Did you know?"

"No!" I guess I looked sufficiently horrified because he relaxed. "I don't have a death wish. Harry told me afterwards.

He had a mild heart attack. My fault." I failed to keep the disgust out of my voice.

Drio didn't try to excuse my behavior or offer platitudes. Setting down the wooden spoon, he wrapped his arms around me and held me tight. "Is he going to be okay with our relationship?"

"Yes, because he loves me. You, on the other hand, he's not too fond of, so expect to be tortured mercilessly."

"He's old. I can take him." He caressed my cheek. "Hey, we can ease into our families if you'd like. My parents'll be cool if we need some time to ourselves before hanging out with them."

"Yeah, I'd like that."

Once the pasta had boiled, Drio made short work of plating it with the sauce in two enormous heaps. He garnished it with a generous amount of freshly grated parmesan and topped it all with some black pepper. "Ecco qua. Buon appetito."

"Bon appetit." I dug in. "Ooh. Spicy. It's delicious."

"Glad you like it."

What I really liked was all these little moments we were gathering, like touchstones moving forward.

We did the dishes in companionable silence. After that sauce, Drio gave me some parsley to get rid of my garlic breath, but I still used half a bottle of his mouthwash after I'd brushed my teeth.

I hung up his robe and slid under the covers with him. His freshly washed sheets smelled lemon-fresh, and his comforter was nice and thick. Warm and cozy, I snuggled into his side. I'd always liked sleeping with Drio because I woke up in his arms. Even if I came half-awake in the middle of the night and he was fast asleep, he would roll in to me and pull me to him.

"Naked and in bed with me every night," he said.

I sighed. "We're going to have to discuss the long-distance thing."

"When did we become long-distance?"

"My life is in Vancouver and yours is here. You have an apartment, friends, a favorite restaurant."

"Bella, I'm Rasha and that meant going wherever I was deployed. You're still in school and all your work is in Vancouver. We can spend summers here or whenever you get a break. Besides, I'm unemployed now. I need to sponge off you."

"Wait. You're not rich? Aw man. This is awkward because I was only in this for your money."

He propped his arm behind his head and stared up at the ceiling. "If you think about it, my lack of a job is all Nava's fault. Which means Ro shares a lot of the blame for encouraging her."

"Right? He should totally foot all your bills."

"We'll add it to your expense account."

I rested my head on his chest. "If he won't, we'll be okay. I have massively cheap rent by Vancouver standards. We'll get by."

"Mmm."

I poked him. "That was pointedly vague. Are you keeping something from me?"

"Here's the thing. I'm not rock star rich, but I'm comfortable. This apartment building has been in our family for generations and when my grandparents died, they left it to me."

"You own this building. Oh, crap. So technically I vandalized your building when I broke the window?"

"Don't worry, I'll bill you." He kissed the tip of my nose. "But I get all the rent from the units, so I'm financially sound."

"I see." I jabbed a finger at him and he caught it between his teeth, nipping it. "You will be paying for all our flights back to Rome while I'm still in school," I said. "Vito will want to see me often, so may I suggest a savings plan?"

"Did I mention I was super cheap? We'll make the Über take us."

I raised my head to look at him. "Huh? What Über goes from Canada to Italy?"

"Nava."

I snorted my laughter. "Omigod. I forgot you called her that. You have a death wish."

"Eh, I have a kickass girlfriend who can take her. I'm good."

I snuggled into the crook of his arm, feeling all warm and ridiculously pleased. Couldn't argue with that.

12

"Arghmhg." I kicked the villain trying to get me out of the nice warm bed.

Drio swore. "You're the one who booked the first flight out. Get up."

I snarled at him, wrestling him for the covers.

"Put the teeth away, my little goblin."

That earned him a pillow flung at his face. "That better not be your new pet name for me."

"How about goblinissima? No? Then move it."

"Threats don't work on me," I said.

"Yeah, I figured that out when you kept ignoring me and doing what you wanted whenever I said I was going to kill you. That's why I bought bribes. Three cornetti and a latte. All yours if you're in the kitchen in five."

I was there in four. I didn't know what cornetti were but I wasn't about to miss out on some new Italian delicacy. "Happy?"

Drio ran his hands over my long-sleeved blue velvet mini dress that I wore with black velvet leggings and gave a satisfied nod. "Missing the jewelry, but much more you. How much stuff did you cram into that bag of yours?"

"Not much. The dress, this change of clothing, my lock

picks, make-up, and energy bars. Enough with the small talk. These cornetti better be worth it."

Drio held up a brown bag. "A little respect, please. I had to get in line before the café opened to get my hands on these. And even then, the only reason I got any that were warm was because I helped the owner with a demon problem a couple years ago. These babies are worth more than gold here in Italy."

"That's a lot of hype, Rossi. You overcompensating again?"

He placed his hand on his heart. "I will not hear you speak poorly of cornetti."

"Yeah, yeah. Show me the goods."

He put three buttery pastries on a plate. They were horn-shaped, lightly glazed, and smelled deliciously of dough with a light dusting of powdered sugar.

I narrowed my eyes. "They're croissants. Italian croissants. You can't fool me, Rasha."

"Take that back. They are far superior."

"Whatever." I bit into the first one. It was filled with pastry cream, and yes, it was still warm. "Flaky, but doesn't fall apart. Rich, sweet." I licked my lips, having become something of a gourmand in all things pastry. "Dough has a bit of a citrus tang to it."

"Weirdo."

"Shut up. I'm appreciating your national cuisine." I took my time with the next two, one filled with Nutella and the final one with almond paste. "For future reference, I will stick with the cream ones and I would like them warm every morning whenever we're in Rome."

"Hell no. I'm not going through that every day."

I brushed my lips against his. "I'll make it worth your while."

"Once a week, and you'll make it worth my while anyway because I'll make it worth yours."

"Four times," I countered.

"Twice."

I blinked adorably at him.

He crossed his arms. "You gonna try and cute your way into a better deal?"

"I mean, if it works. Did it work?"

"We'll discuss it after we see the Appraiser."

The flight to Antwerp was fairly routine: Drio fell asleep on my shoulder halfway through and then woke up cranky, rubbing his eyes like a little kid when I nudged him on our final descent. When we exited the airport, thunderous dark clouds pressed in on us, but they couldn't dim the charm of this medieval port city.

A stunning gothic cathedral dominated the skyline and winding cobblestone lanes were packed with cafés. The city was surprisingly multicultural. According to our taxi driver, there were vibrant Jewish, Indian, Arab, and Chinese communities. In fact, this was Belgium's only officially recognized Chinatown with the entrance to the neighborhood marked by an elaborate pagoda gate in blue, red, and gold.

The Appraiser's shop was located a few blocks off the edge of the Diamond Quarter, its windows filled to bursting with bling. Massive rings shaped like wolf skulls with diamonds for eyes, ostentatious engagement rings, a Hello Kitty made of diamonds—my demon side was in gem heaven. Fine. Not just her. I debated how best to add a $300,000 black diamond ring that was studded with smaller diamonds to my expense account but couldn't think of any creative line item to cover the cost. I eyed my flash-stepping boyfriend, then sighed. Asking him to commit robbery for me when we'd just gotten together might be a bit much. Maybe for our six-month anniversary.

We presented ourselves to the intercom camera and got buzzed into a tiny space. Only once the outer doors had locked were we buzzed through a second set of doors and into the shop itself.

A familiar older blonde woman sat on a tall stool behind a counter filled with yet more diamond jewelry. Her blue eyes were dull. I frowned. Usually, she was cheerier, glad to see me, not this listless attendant polishing a bracelet. "You have her gift?"

"Yes." I cocked my head. "Are you feeling okay?"

The woman laughed nervously, her breathing shallow. "I'm fine."

She clearly wasn't, but we all had bad days. I wasn't going to press it, even if Drio's brow did furrow.

The employee opened up the pass-through in the counter and motioned us to the back. "Go in." She hit a buzzer, allowing us through yet another door.

I wrinkled my nose at the strong smell of salami that hit us from the back room, but was quickly distracted.

Jewelers' tools and loose diamonds cluttered the metal table that took up most of the space. My demon blinked her eyes open in unholy glee and I stuffed my hands in my pockets, because the Appraiser would show her wrath if I "liberated" any of these gems and I didn't have any of my usual mass of bracelets with me. Thanks to Harry's drills, my jewelry kept me grounded and myself in situations like these. I could do it on my own without them, like I was doing now, it was just harder.

A spiral staircase in one corner led to a loft area with her living quarters. I wasn't sure she actually ever left the store.

Drio's blank expression upon first seeing the Appraiser was a testament to his training. The half-goblin was easily six-feet-tall and skinny as a rake, so far removed from human society that her name was lost in the mists. Her hair was a rat's nest explosion of red and her skin was pale enough for her fine blue veins to pop like vibrant threads.

None of that was the surprising part. No, that honor went to her long warty nose and pointed ears that she didn't bother to glamour anymore. The story I'd heard was that she'd struggled to integrate into regular human society, failed, and left a promising career as a bio-chemist about thirty years ago to hole up in this room to work with diamonds.

I'd always felt a bit smug around the Appraiser. My humanity reigned strong and I had friends and family, not just the allure of cold, hard gems. Today, however, I saw her through Drio's eyes, a shambles of a creature living in the cracks.

My fate if I lost the battle with my redcap.

Half-goblins didn't live any longer than regular people, and I was one of the ones who didn't glamour because my human body was all I had. Was that why I'd chosen Team Human? That it wasn't some great morality and connection to the human race on my part, that it was simply because I looked human, therefore I could pass? Would my life, my choices have been different had I resembled the Appraiser? Would my otherness have been too foreign, even with the ability to glamour, leaving me holed up and alone, not even a full goblin, and therefore not comfortable in their tightly-knit communities, either?

Much as I wished I could decisively declare that of course I still would have made the same decisions, right now, I wasn't actually sure.

Drio scanned the room, not paying me any attention, but he had to be comparing me to her. It was one thing to be a half-demon in a cute human package, but there was no illusion of humanity before us. I'd always stayed one hundred percent human because letting even a sliver of my otherness poke through was risky. Standing here now, I couldn't believe that I'd ever considered some kind of truce with my inner demon. I blamed sex brain.

The Appraiser was packing up a velvet pouch and didn't appear to notice us, but I wasn't fooled. She knew we were here and had already assessed us for possible threats. It was up to me to proffer my gift before she'd deign to deal with us.

Moving very slowly with exaggerated movements, I retrieved the Rust from my bra and set it on the counter. Then I stepped back.

The half-demon reached for the Rust. Stopped herself. Reached once more. Pinched the inside of her wrist, muttering.

Drio shot me an unimpressed stare.

"Appraiser?" I said. "Can you examine our items?"

She sent a final longing glance at the Rust, then nodded brusquely. Gift accepted. Business would commence.

I handed her the Tupperware containing the ring and the iron bar. She sat down on a tall stool, and flicked on a bright lamp to get a first impression through the transparent container. Clicking her tongue, she snapped on a pair of gloves and opened the lid.

Removing the ring, she examined the diamond through a jeweler's loupe. She sniffed it, she licked it.

"Any idea what demon sent it?" Drio said.

"No." Her voice was papery and rough with disuse.

"Then what can you tell us?" He crossed his arms, rustling his worn leather jacket.

Her hand flexed on empty air, just shy of the vial of Rust.

"Appraiser," I said sternly. There was a protocol to our visits. I presented the Rust, we did our business, and only once it was concluded did she use the drug. Her addiction had escalated.

I shifted, blocking her view of the vial.

Twitching, she grabbed a metal canister similar to a paint can from the floor and pried open the lid. Liquid nitrogen smoke curled out.

I leaned forward, curious to see what she was going to do with the ring.

In a blur of motion, she elbowed me aside, grabbed the Rust, and plunged the vial into the liquid nitrogen with her bare hand that was covered in pink patches of new skin growth.

Drio didn't move but the air charged with a new alertness.

The glass on the vial cracked and the half-demon gave a low, satisfied growl. When she pulled her hand out, it glowed green. The Rust had been absorbed into her skin. Foam bubbled at the corner of her mouth, and she flicked out a fleshy tongue to wipe her lips clean.

I barely suppressed my shudder.

"Good quality." Her voice was hoarse and her pupils were dilated. Then her head lolled forward and she slumped over the table.

"This is pointless," Drio said to me in a low voice. "She's a junkie demon who can't help us."

"No, the Appraiser is a half-demon using it when the noise in her head gets overwhelming. Rust reboots her brain. She'll wake up with a sharp clarity that helps her focus. She needs it."

His expression turned thunderous. "You know this how?"

"Because I'm good at my job." I gave him a humorless smile. "What did you think?"

Say it. I dare you.

He presented his best poker face in response. "She's so far gone that she doesn't care if we see her use."

"She's managing her addiction best she can."

"Yeah." Drio jerked a finger at her, face down on the table, a contemptuous look on his face. "Really got it under control. Look at her hands. They've been burned and had to regenerate skin so many times, you can read them like tree trunk rings. She's been out of her mind so long that she can barely remember how to talk."

The Appraiser jolted up. "Leave."

"No problem," he said.

I grabbed his arm. "No. You are the only one who can give us answers. He's sorry. Apologize," I hissed at Drio.

A muscle ticked in Drio's jaw. "I'm sorry."

The Appraiser pointed at the door.

No, no, no. This visit had gone sideways in record time, and I was about to lose the case. I brought my hands together in supplication. "Please, Appraiser."

"It will cost you."

Fucking Rasha arrogance. Had it just been me, I would have had my answers with the Rust. Now I'd have to get answers the other way.

"The usual deal?" I asked. She nodded, eyes still cagey as I sighed then rolled up my velvet sleeve. As much as I tried to live as a human, there were some things that I would never be truly free of. I could choose to run from who I was or embrace it and use it to help me. I took a breath and steeled myself, then laid my wrist vein-side-up on the metal table.

Drio's eyes narrowed, widened, but by the time he lunged for me, it was too late.

The Appraiser's canines elongated into sharp points and closed on my skin.

My nostrils filled with the hot tang of blood and the world turned vague and dim, drenched in red. My goblin side wrenched free of her shackles, demanding that same right to feed.

Je nourris. Tu nourris. Elle nourrit. I chanted the words under my breath. My white light wavered, her darkness taking form.

I feed. You feed. She feeds. Hear me, I am human. Take your blood urges and shove them.

Darkness had blotted out more than half of the light inside me. My goblin flexed her muscles, primed and ready to take me on and overthrow me.

"Enough," I growled and wrenched my hand away.

The Appraiser licked my blood off her lips.

I grabbed a chocolate banana protein bar from my jacket pocket, fumbling to open the wrapper, but my fingers didn't want to work properly.

Drio took it away from me, tearing the package open and putting a chunk to my mouth.

I barely chewed it, white-knuckling the edge of the metal table. The underside was sharp, biting into my skin. I drew the pain inside, letting it cut through the red haze that filled my vision. At least the bleeding had stopped, the puncture wounds sealed.

Drio fed me the rest of the bar and then a second one.

I wanted to thank Drio and I wanted to bite his fingers off. Rage hurtled through me and I clamped my lips together so I wouldn't scream. *This is what happens when I truly don't hold back. This is what's waiting for you. Do you still want it? Are you happy now?*

I banished my demon, my chest rising and falling in jagged breaths, then went to the sink and washed my wrist off. Just because I'd done a blood trade didn't mean I wanted someone else's spit and my own dried blood on my arm all day. Gross.

Drio was strung tight, holding it together by sheer force of will power.

I started to place my hand on his chest, then dropped it to my side. He didn't get comfort. He'd put me in this position.

"I paid the price willingly," I said.

"You did." The Appraiser took the ring to another workstation across the room. Using a small butane torch, she heated it, then dropped it in a mason jar of clear liquid. She gave a startled laugh, like a rusty car door closing, and pulled out the wet ring with a pair of tongs. "This isn't a diamond."

"It's synthetic?" I said.

"It's a synthetic casing, but it goes beyond that. Real diamonds have inclusions. The most common are pinpoints, which are like tiny black dots. Then there are feather inclusions, small cracks and holes like a tooth cavity. Synthetic diamonds are flawless. This was glamoured to look flawless, but it's far from that." Still holding the ring by the tongs, she brought the ring over to us.

I yelped at the black mass that ebbed and flowed within the heart of the jewel.

"Porco Dio," Drio said.

"Was this the thing compelling them?" I said.

"More likely the reason they were compelled." The Appraiser placed the ring and the bar on a slide under a large, high-powered microscope with some weird Frankenstein knobs and rods attached to it. She adjusted them, clicking her tongue, then hunched over and looked into the eyepiece lens. The green glow on her hand was fading, replaced by raw, red blisters from the liquid nitrogen.

"The bar and ring form a circuit, siphoning off magic from whomever possesses the items," she said.

"Could that be any random person with magic?" I said.

She straightened up with a cracking sound, one hand on her back. "No. The diamond represents the circle and requires feminine magic. The bar is the male. Needs a Rasha."

I'd held out hope that Drio's involvement wasn't deliberate. Now I knew. It was targeted from the start.

"What were we powering?" Drio watched the black mass shifting hypnotically in random patterns inside the diamond. "What is that?"

The Appraiser picked up the ring and put it to her ear. Her expression went soft and dreamy. "The Executioner is coming for you."

13

Whether it was the drugs or some ring-induced trance, the Appraiser wouldn't answer any more questions. She also wouldn't return the diamond, holding it to her chest and cooing, "Beware the blood."

Drio flashed over to her and froze. His forehead wrinkled and he balled up one fist, glancing at me. Then with a half-swallowed curse, he slammed his hand on her left hip and fired his Rasha magic into her.

She gasped and disappeared in a shower of gold dust, dead.

His eyes met mine. I dropped the hand I'd been rubbing over my own left hip. "You killed my contact."

"I couldn't leave her alive." He brushed gold dust out of his hair and I tried not to flinch. "She'd been feeding off her employee. The woman was sweaty, pale, and her lips were blue. Classic blood loss symptoms."

Fine. He'd saved a human, but he'd killed a half-demon in front of me like it was nothing. No, that wasn't fair. It had bothered him and that was almost worse.

"You kill demons," I said. "I've killed them, too. We're good on that score."

"Yeah? Then why were you shielding your kill spot?" He

gave a bitter laugh. "How long until you see me as a monster for doing my job? Or one of us gets hurt because I hesitate, worried about the optics of killing them in front of you?"

What was I supposed to say? I shoved the ring and the iron bar back in the Tupperware. "The feeding off her employee wasn't happening last time I was here. I would never have let the Appraiser live if she was doing that."

"But feeding off you was okay?"

"Considering you and Isabella were birthing something called 'the Executioner,' I'd say knowing that was worth the trade-off."

"And if she'd fed off you for thirty seconds longer? Would we be standing here arguing or would I have lost you to your redcap side entirely?"

Something inside me snapped. I flung my words like a barbed spear, piercing everything that had sprung up between us. "Guess a goblin wouldn't look as good on your arm as a pretty witch, huh?"

"Are you fucking kidding me?" he roared.

Shame roiled through me, but I tamped it down and faced him, unabashed. "I always stopped her in time."

Drio sucked in a sharp breath, his expression icing over. Without a word, he spun on his heels and stalked out.

I scrubbed my hand over my face and took a deep breath, letting it out slowly. When that didn't help, I kicked the table. The Tupperware skittered to the edge, but I caught it before it hit the ground. Best not to make any jarring movements with something called an executioner.

Drio was speaking to the employee in a quiet voice, one hand on her shoulder. She nodded, then hugged him, her eyes moist.

We stayed with her until her friend came and got her.

Drio didn't speak to me all the way back to the airport for our return flight to Rome, nor was a single word exchanged through the boarding process or while buckling into our seats. Drio stared resolutely ahead.

Maybe we should just declare this relationship impossible and move on. Rasha were trained to view the world in black-and-white absolutes. He had clung to that in the wake of Asha's murder, single-handedly killing his way through the demon population, though he'd come a long way in moving to an understanding of the world as shades of gray.

Yet, given what had happened with the Appraiser, he obviously had a way to go. He'd made a very prejudiced assumption about how to treat her based on her addiction. Instead of handling the situation with sensitivity and responding appropriately, he'd reverted back to a mindset that only saw in absolutes.

To be fair, hunters didn't need to be sensitive. They tracked and they killed. Game over. My world was different and required a great deal of patience. Sometimes my job was force-based, but often I walked a tightrope, negotiating with various deadly parties where it was imperative to remain tuned in to the tiniest mood or nuanced shift in behavior.

I had to know when to submit and how to enforce my boundaries and survive. That idea was inconceivable to hunters. They were the dominants and they moved through the world accordingly. I wasn't sure we could cross that gulf. Or any of the gulfs that separated us. I sighed, my eyes sliding sideways to see what Drio was doing.

He was watching me.

Did I want this relationship at the cost of having to constantly educate him about my world and his behavior in it? Would he want it if being with me interfered with his ability to kill demons? My temples throbbed. It all sounded exhausting.

The flight attendant made her take-off announcement to strap in and turn off our devices.

The plane began to taxi.

Even though we were the only two people in our row and the rumble of the aircraft drowned out the conversations in the rows around us, Drio leaned into me, his voice low. "My reaction earlier when the Appraiser fed off you had nothing to do with you being a half-goblin. I was shocked that you'd willingly put yourself in danger like that before."

I flipped angrily through the magazine provided in our seat pocket, pretending to be engrossed in an article about Bangkok's waterfront. "What a crazy concept, *Rasha*."

"I didn't say it was rational." He sliced his hand through the air like he was trying to conjure up the right words. "It wasn't even about that. I was disgusted that *I* was the arrogant fuck who put you in that situation today. It wasn't easy for me to admit that to myself. I compromised the work you had done to get us to this point and forced you into a dangerous choice and I'm deeply sorry."

Judging him to be sincere, I put my magazine back in the pocket. "Thank you for owning up to that. I accept your apology."

Our silence was tempered, no longer sharp-edged but still strained. Did I owe him an apology for not prepping him in more depth for what to expect? No. This was still my job. I'd allowed him to come along because he needed to feel active, but he should have kept his mouth shut until we were clear of that situation. I turned over my actions in my head. How would I have responded if he'd let a demon feed off of him? If he'd behaved in a way completely outside my expectations of him?

"The first time I let the Appraiser feed off me was in exchange for a blood ruby after an incident in a South American village last year." I twisted my fingers tightly.

Drio trapped my hands between his, squeezing them briefly with a smile that was so small I almost didn't catch it. My shoulders relaxed a fraction. He nodded at me to continue, stroking my hands in a soothing motion. "Villa de Cama?"

"Villa de Cama was the village where the demons slaughtered everyone. The Rasha who'd killed them were burying the dead when a doctor with Médecins Sans Frontières stumbled in from the jungle, half-delirious and raving that the place he'd been stationed had been turned to stone. An even smaller place. Barely a blip on the map. The Rasha verified the same demons had been responsible, then called Harry, unsure of what to do."

"Isn't Harry just a go-between to get to you, the informant for the Vancouver chapter?"

"No, Harry did a lot of jobs for the Brotherhood. That's how I got involved."

"Hold on." Drio frowned. "I read about that one. The one where those people remained frozen even after the demons were killed?"

"Unusual, right? That's why the Rasha were stymied. Harry called in some favors and learned about a blood ruby that would do the trick of unfreezing them."

The plane hit a bout of turbulence and my stomach dropped into my toes.

"You were sent to the Appraiser to trade your blood so she'd give up the gem," he said.

"PD blood is the most sought-after vintage, dontcha know," I drawled, pointedly using the term that Rasha had coined for half-demons. *What do you call a half-demon? Practice.* "A delightful blend of the most mouthwatering properties of human and demon blood."

His nostrils flared. "Harry pimped you out for your blood."

"He gave me a choice."

"That's not a choice. It's emotional blackmail. He appealed to your decency knowing full well what decision you'd make."

I jerked my hands away. "By that logic, being Rasha is an unending series of caving to emotional blackmail. No, wait. It's slavery because once that hamsa ring is on your finger, you don't even have a choice. You do what they tell you. Don't belittle my decision-making abilities or my intelligence. I'm not a damsel in distress. If we're going to be together, you need to trust my read of a situation and that I know what I'm doing. Even if you don't understand the reasons, that doesn't mean there aren't any or that they aren't damn good ones. And ultimately, you have to accept that you can have my back, but if you can't respect who I am and what I do, this is over."

"I swear I do respect you and your decisions. I'm in awe of you. It's just hard for me. Not an excuse. I know I have to do better."

"Up here, you respect me." I tapped my head. "But can you deal with it here?" I tapped my heart.

He kissed my knuckles. "Yes, because the alternative of not having you in my life is unthinkable. Letting people we love head into the fire is not an easy concept for Rasha."

"I know."

"I will be the man who deserves you." He spoke it like a vow.

I wished that in return, I could say that I'd find a way to reconcile both sides of myself and be whole. For him. For myself. But I was too raw, so I went with humor. I brushed my lips against his. "And I'll be the woman who lets you deserve me."

Drio laughed. "Grazie. Finish your story. What happened with the blood ruby?"

"It was used in the ritual and the villagers were saved."

"How many more times have you been fed off?" he asked softly.

"Just once before today, and again it was with her. It sounds crazy but I trusted the Appraiser. She was half-redcap like me and she was careful, in her way. Redcaps can drain as slowly or as quickly as they like, and she was experienced enough to have established some control. She never went so fast that I was unable to stop her."

I pulled out the ring and held it to my ear like the Appraiser had.

There was the faint sound of wind, rushing through leaves.

I switched the ring to my other ear, but I wasn't imagining

the sound. I put the diamond against Drio's ear like a seashell. "Listen."

"Wind." He frowned. "That reminds me of something."

"A demon trait?" I secured the ring back in its Tupperware and put it in my purse.

"Yeah." He pulled out his phone to connect to Ada but this small plane didn't have an internet option. He tapped his thumb against the screen.

Our flight attendant came by to offer us a non-alcoholic beverage. This day had been a shitshow and pop wasn't going to cut it. I thanked her and refused the offer, though I accepted the complimentary pretzels.

Drio refused the drink and the snack.

"He'll take the pretzels, thanks." The package crinkled, the tiny pretzels barely even a decent mouthful. "We're all clear now?" I said, once the attendant had moved on.

"Your call, your body, your case," he said.

"You mean that or are you going to freak out if this ever happens again?"

"I'd rather you don't bleed on my behalf in the future, but I'll respect your decisions."

"Get over yourself. I was doing this for Isabella." I shook the last of the pretzels into my mouth and started in on the second package.

He pressed his hands to his heart, a mock-wounded expression on his face. "Unlike that undercover job you were on a few months ago, you didn't cuff me and take off to deal with the demon on your own so if you think about it, we're making huge leaps and bounds."

"I cuffed you *twice* when I was after that ala. Oh, the dumbfounded look on your face." I pretended to wipe a tear from my eye.

"Cazzo." Drio jerked upright. "Ala demons. They turn themselves into black wind. They only stay in human form when hunting and eating children," he said sourly. "But hey, they're not Italian."

"Yes, fine. You get to say 'I told you so.' They're also storm demons that could easily trap you for a week." These dry-ass pretzels were a drop in the unending sea of my hunger. I grabbed the menu card from the seat pocket to inspect my choices.

"What if this is revenge on me for killing that other ala? What was her name?" He waggled his fingers like it could access his memory. "Ally."

Ugh. Everything here was uninspiring and overpriced and not more cornetti. I shoved the stupid menu at Drio. "Antonia is going to curse the hell out of you."

Drio choked out a laugh and put the menu away. "She can get in line behind this second ala."

I jotted down notes on my phone. "Is the Executioner that black mass or is it the demon who compelled the ring?"

Drio shrugged. "If it's an ala, then what is that mass and what were Isabella and I supposed to do with it?"

My fingers flew over the keyboard. "Also, what's the blood we need to beware of, beyond its obvious connection as source of dark magic rituals?"

Drio winced. "The wedding. It was going to take place on October 31st."

"All Hallows' Eve. A night of great power for demons and a night dedicated to human sacrifice. I hope you guys were really going to embrace the theme," I said. "The appetizer opportunities alone would have been stellar. Entrails on potato crusti with red pepper jelly, dirty martinis with pickled eyeballs."

"Do a Dead Velvet Cake in a red sauce, maybe some Bloody Marys." He scratched his chin. "Sorry, this is Italy. Bloody Marias. Stash all the Marias behind the bar and mainline it right out of them."

"I'm almost sorry I ruined your plans. That would have been something to see."

"You assume you were invited," Drio scoffed.

I punched his arm and he chuckled.

"You and Isabella power up that black windy mass," I said. "And because it's under a glamour, you have no idea it exists. It feeds off you for three weeks and then on Halloween, at your wedding, it what?"

"Breaks free of the ring? If the thing in the diamond is an extension of this ala demon, then it wipes everyone at the wedding out."

I frowned at our list of questions and speculation. "That's a lot of work to Red Wedding your nuptials."

"Parties like that don't just throw themselves," Drio said.

"Even so. Why have you marry anyone? Is it really as simple as bringing all the people you care about in a room together so that this mass could be released and kill you?"

"Sure. That's a solid demon revenge plan."

"Then answer this. Why marry a stranger?" I shook my head. We were missing something.

"What if it wasn't supposed to be a stranger?" he said. "What if it was supposed to be someone I cared about?"

I didn't whine "why wasn't it me," but Drio squeezed my hand. "The demon might not have known you had any magic of your own," he said.

Oh. That could be true.

I snapped my fingers. "Nava. The night of Rohan's show she asked me if I was picking up any stalker vibes. What if the second ala was there that night and planned to use her originally but he or she didn't have the opportunity? Not to mention Rohan's slavish devotion to Nee the night of the performance might have kiboshed her usefulness. Why set a very angry Rasha determined to get his girlfriend back on your trail? The demon needed a new pawn."

"Enter Isabella." Drio swiped the pretzel bag away and ate the last couple of salty snacks.

I almost lunged at him because dry or not, that was the last of our snacks, but he was kinda cute, gesturing and crinkling the bag as he spoke, and besides, he'd already swallowed the pretzels. He could live.

"If the ala was monitoring me somehow," he said, "he would have known where I was going and why."

"That answers the question of how it had time to put this all into place. It was already in place before Ro's performance. The demon just switched out one of the players," I said.

"It sure as hell kept tabs on me. Isabella was a large part of my conversation with Antonia. It wasn't just about convincing her to allow the training facility, it was to allow Isabella to train as a hunter." Drio stretched out his long legs, squashing them under the seat in front of him.

The flight attendant came on over the speaker system, asking everyone to place our seats in the upright position and fasten our seat belts for landing.

"You think it's still incubating?" Drio cast a wary glance at my purse.

"I think we need an old-school witch with a lot of magic and lore at her fingertips to tell us."

Drio slouched down in his seat. "I knew you were going to say that."

***

ANTONIA THREW up her hands at the sight of us, but she didn't bandy about giant ice blocks, so this was already miles ahead of last time. "Allora. Come."

She led us into a huge kitchen painted a cheery yellow. Braided strands of garlic hung to dry on one wall and a neat row of small ceramic planters held a variety of herbs on the windowsill.

A bowl of bright lemons sat on the counter next to a pile of partially rolled out dough.

Antonia opened her freezer, withdrew a container, and slammed it on the table. "I suppose you want coffee."

Isabella, wearing these cool slouchy jeans and an off-the-shoulder top, her hair tied back in a simple bun at her neck, dried her hands on a tea towel and motioned for Drio and me to sit down.

We took the farthest seats from Antonia, who was banging around the room.

"Well?" Antonia pointed her rolling pin at us. "Did you get the demon or do I turn you into frogs?"

"That's not actually a thing," I said. "You end up with a green tinge or flippers, but there's no total transformation."

Antonia paused over the dough, lips pursed, and then looked at me with narrowed eyes. "How do you know?"

"Nava Katz is my best friend."

"I should curse her as well." She lay into the dough with such force that the flour she'd dusted the counter with flew up in a cloud.

Isabella ran the espresso machine, presenting us with two jewel-colored cups of dark brew. "Hear them out, Nonna."

I switched my blue cup for Drio's green one, because I wanted the one that matched his eyes.

He shook his head at me, a small smile hovering on his lips, then clinked his cup to mine. "Salut."

Isabella opened the lid on the container to reveal a variety of cookies. "Please help yourselves."

I explained everything we'd learned, while dedicating myself to sampling every flavor of cookie. The round lemon ones were the best, though the crinkly almond ones were pretty good. I didn't care for the short biscotti with the raisins. Why ruin perfectly good biscotti that way?

Drio apparently agreed, because he pushed the raisin ones to one side of the container where they wouldn't touch the others he was scarfing down.

Antonia's rolling grew less poundy and there were longer and longer pauses between rolls. "You endangered my granddaughter. Set this Executioner after her."

"Not on purpose, but yes. Mi dispiace," Drio said.

Her dough went up in flames.

"No hunting ever," Antonia pronounced. "And you." She pointed at me. "The only good demon is a dead one."

Her rolling pin whizzed through the air like a spear.

Drio flashed out, but Antonia flicked her fingers at him and he flashed right back in, rooted to the floor.

I flung my chair at the pin, but it cut through the seat, aimed straight at my head. One of the few times I wished I had full demon magic.

Right before it impaled me, a blast splintered the pin into fragments that fell harmlessly at my feet.

"You're as bad as your father," Isabella said, shaking her hands out.

Antonia vibrated with fury, shoving the burned dough into the garbage. She was about to light into Isabella when I cut her off.

"Let's not say things we'll regret later." I kicked the curls of wood into a neat pile. Negotiation: another crucial P.I. skill and one that was very rapidly coming in handy as Drio and I navigated being trapped between two very angry and hot-headed Italian witches. Honestly, at this point, I was more concerned the most damage they would do would be to each other.

Free to move again, Drio edged over to me. He stepped in front of me like a shield, thought about it a moment, then repositioned himself so he was next to me, shoring up my left side. Well, well. The boy could learn.

"You can't hide your head in the sand," I said. "Not about hunting and not about this. You're a leader, Antonia, so lead. Do you have any knowledge of the black mass? Can we destroy it?"

Antonia slammed her hand on the counter. It cracked like gunfire.

Isabella, Drio, and I flinched.

She snorted out a breath like a bull, and wiped her hands on her apron. "Give me the artifacts."

I retrieved the Tupperware and placed it on the table.

Antonia removed the ring. The black mass continued its shifting patterns inside the diamond, with no visible change to its size or color. She pricked her finger with a small paring knife, allowing a single drop of blood to fall on the jewel as she engulfed the ring in magic.

The mass broke into various smaller pieces that bumped around inside the diamond.

"The Executioner is the demon." She tapped the ring. "This is the weapon."

"What is it?" Isabella said.

"A magic virus fed by blood. If you're correct about the wedding, then its contagion period was timed to that night. Everyone who shook hands with either Drio or Isabella would have been infected and dead before the cake was cut." Antonia smacked Drio across the top of his head. "Ma come sei cosi stupido?"

"I'd have been stupid if I'd done this on purpose," he ground out. "Which I did not."

"That's a solid revenge plan." I swallowed. "Shit."

Antonia raised her hand at me.

"What did I do?"

"Language." She fixed those scary eyes on me like she was boring straight into my soul and seeing every transgression I'd ever committed.

"Can you destroy the virus?" I said.

Antonia twirled her hand in the air like I was seriously pissing her off and engulfed the ring in magic for a very long time. The black masses faded and then disappeared entirely.

I poked the ring and iron bar. "I don't feel any magic in them anymore. They're clean."

"Boh. Of course, they're clean," Antonia scoffed.

"What if this Executioner is able to compel these things again?" Isabella said. "Compel us? This ala is after Drio and I was caught in the crossfire, but if I'd been trained to protect myself, to fight like witches were supposed to, maybe I could have avoided this." She stood up defiantly. "I'm not going to cower. If you won't allow the training facility here in Rome, Nonna, I'll go somewhere else. I refuse to be helpless any longer."

Scowling, Antonia pulled a second rolling pin out of a drawer. Whoa. How many of these things did she go through? Maybe that's how she'd held on to her position for so long. Death by rolling pin. I imagined a deep movie voice giving the tagline, "She finished the cookies. Now it's your turn."

"I was raised to believe that hunters were a higher law," Drio said, taking the rolling pin from her and putting it safely on the counter. "The ultimate morality, answerable to no one other than the Brotherhood. It didn't occur to me to question that the world might be bigger, wider, and more complex. Women taught me how wrong I was." He smiled at me. "Women like Isabella, and like you, Antonia, are an important part of the equation. We need you. All of you, because these demons aren't going to stop coming. Trust me, I know how hard it is to let someone you care about face that kind of evil, but don't clip Isabella's wings. Let her soar."

"Are there more like him?" Isabella asked me.

"I think this one's unique," I said.

Drio shot me a smug look and heat curled down my spine.

Mate, my goblin re-iterated.

I clamped both hands over my mouth to make sure I hadn't said it out loud. How embarrassing. Sure, I recognized that slow and steady wasn't the right play anymore, but come on, I was acting like a high schooler convinced she'd met the person she was going to marry. This wasn't how I did things.

But my goblin kept saying it with such certainty, I almost wondered–

Nope. Stopping there. While I grappled with these earth-shaking pronouncements, Antonia was studying her grand-daughter.

A flash of resignation and then pride touched her features.

The steely glint returned to her eyes. "Va bene. The training center may proceed."

"Can I hunt?" Isabella said.

Antonia nodded. Isabella squealed and hugged her grandmother. Antonia endured it for a moment, then patted her granddaughter's back and disentangled herself. It reminded me of Ari with Nava and I tamped down on a grin.

"Antonia, can you destroy the artifacts? No artifacts, no way to compel Drio and Isabella," I said.

She fired her magic directly into the heart of the diamond. The ring shattered into dust, with the iron bar soon following.

I breathed a sigh of relief. "Thank you. Crisis averted."

Isabella and Drio let out gasping wheezes, the sound a bagpipe would make if it were shot. A black mass about the size of my hand slithered under both their skins like an animated tattoo.

Antonia clutched Isabella's shoulders with a surprising strength, pretty much the only thing keeping her granddaughter upright. Healing magic pulsed out of her hands.

I pushed up Drio's sleeves to touch his bare skin and streamed my magic inside him, praying it would be enough to keep him stable until Antonia could get to him with the full force of her power.

Antonia knocked my hand away. "No magic. Not even healing. It feeds."

All the worst things did.

Isabella swayed, catching hold of the counter. The mass had doubled in size, crawling over her skin.

"You destroyed the virus," I said. "Magic should kill it."

"It's inside them now." Antonia wrung her hands. "Mutated to the next stage."

Fuck!

Drio sagged sideways and I barely caught him, his chair tipping back.

"Does it hurt?" I said.

"Just dizzy."

"I need to lie down." Isabella stumbled out of the kitchen.

Antonia hurried after her, guiding her down the hallway.

"That's a good idea." Drio slid so far off his chair that he was hanging on by his tailbone.

"Keep your ass in that chair." I shoved him mostly upright with my shoulder.

Antonia returned, ashen. "I can't lose her and I can't leave her. I'm trusting you, you understand?"

"I won't fail you, I swear," I said. "Is there anything we can do for them magic-wise?"

She sagged, and I was aware for the first time of how frail she actually was. "Find this Executioner and kill him."

"At least we have time," I said, desperately looking for a bright side. "It's still a couple of weeks until Halloween."

Antonia pulled me aside, not that Drio was in any condition to eavesdrop. His eyes were glazed and his head was slowly falling forward. "We don't have that long. The virus is feeding directly off them and not via a circuit. It has free rein on its energy source."

As if to underscore her point, a slithering patch broke free from the main mass to run along one side of Drio's neck.

"How long do we have before this virus–" I swallowed "–can no longer be stopped?"

"Best guess? Three days."

14

Antonia portalled us back to my apartment so we would be in Vancouver with our friends close by to help. I'd barely gotten Drio into the bedroom before he collapsed, sprawled face-down on my mattress.

Grunting, I pushed him onto his back.

He fluttered his hand out for me. "Don't go. I just need a minute."

I sat down on the bed, smoothing his hair out of his face. "Yeah. Maybe a nap?"

His hair fell like silk through my fingers, mesmerizing me. I unbuttoned his shirt, cataloguing where the unblemished skin along his torso met the dark shifting streaks on his abs.

"I heard her," he said. "Three days."

"Pfft. Plenty of time to find the demon." I settled a pillow under his head, pulled off his shoes, and adjusted the blankets around him. The tendril of satisfied possessiveness that bloomed inside me at the sight of him in my bed warred with the icy fingers squeezing my chest. Any doubts or frustration I'd had with Drio or with our situation had fled.

"Now." I sat back against the headboard, pressed up next to him and unlocked my phone. "Pay attention, Rossi. I'm about to let you peer behind the curtain and into the secrets of private investigating."

It was the exact same process he used as a hunter, but I needed to keep him with me and banter was as good a plan as any.

His lids fluttered close. "Sure thing, Oz."

"That's Great and Powerful Oz to you." I logged into Ada. "First, we check for any mention of an Executioner." I typed it into the database as I spoke. "No results. Really?" I frowned at my screen. "I would have thought that would be a popular moniker."

"Go figure," Drio said.

I opened the container on the table next to my bed that was filled with dried fruits and nuts for when I was binge watching on my laptop in bed and needed a high energy snack. "Luckily, we in the P.I. business are fleet of foot and capable of changing our investigative track in a nanosecond. "Plugging keywords 'ala' and 'virus' in. Go."

I scarfed back a good three-quarters of the mix while Ada processed the search. Every bite clogged my throat like dust, but now more than ever, I had to stay alert and in control. There was no room for mistakes.

"Nothing from either the witch or Rasha intel about ala demons ever creating viruses," I said. "They control storms, they turn into a black wind, but viruses, not so much. A minion maybe? No. This virus would take a more powerful and precise ability."

"Two demons," Drio said.

"Possibly. Or we're on the wrong path with the ala." I widened the search to demons in general. "Wait. This seems promising. A black wind that devours everything in its path."

"The tornado controlled by the demon Pazuzu," Drio said. "Who was killed three hundred years ago."

"Shoot. You're right."

Eyes still closed, Drio smirked at me.

"Smug and bedridden is not a good look, Rossi."

My search hit a dead end. There was no mention of which demons were capable of creating viruses or had created them in the past.

Drio hadn't spoken in a while. I reached for his chest, then pulled my hand away.

"Still breathing," he said.

"Remote logging in to work and accessing my case files now." I scrolled backwards through the documents until I hit the relevant one. "My notes on Ally. I'd compiled a pretty comprehensive profile on her before I befriended her."

"You stalked her," he murmured.

"Obviously." I read my notes aloud. Most of it was regarding her child-hunting patterns, but I had also noted everyone she associated with, along with transcripts of our conversations. "Here we go. Ally mentioned a new guy she was seeing. Derek Brown."

"Human or demon?"

"Demon. At the time I suspected Brown was a diwrmach, which means with the right incentive he'll be open to talking. I'm going to have to leave you for a bit but I'll be back soon." I pressed his hand to my heart, a swell of emotion propelling the words out of me. "Cuore–"

"Don't." He tried to sit up, an angry look on his face, but he was too weak. "Don't say it out of pity." His words were slurred.

"Hot, smart, fucks like a god. Yeah, you got me. It's definitely pity."

A smile ghosted his lips, though his eyes didn't open.

I called Nava and explained the situation in a low voice. "Can you or Ro come stay with him, please? I need to go in to the office."

"One sec."

Through the phone came the sound of breaking glass, followed by a loud growl, Nava swearing, and Rohan's grunt.

"I'm back," she said.

"Do I want to know?"

They popped into the apartment. Rohan's shirt was slashed and Nava had a black eye. "Demon," she said. "Taken care of."

They moved closer to the bed, watching Drio sleep.

Rohan's lips flattened. "It's a fail-safe. That fucking Executioner made sure that even if the ring and bar were destroyed that his plan would be carried out. The virus would be embedded in Drio and Isabella."

"I'm not convinced an ala demon is behind all this," I said. "There could be two demons. The ala to deal with the storm and then another one for the virus."

"What's the motivation for the second one?" Rohan said.

"I don't know? Revenge for something else?"

"With Drio's love of killing spawn?" Nava said. "That could be a very long list."

"There's another thing I'm struggling with," I said. "The method of vengeance. If I was going to avenge someone, my plot would involve maximum hurt on every level: physical, emotional, and psychological. The virus ticks the physical box, and maybe even the emotional one, because Drio would know he was responsible for killing everyone before he bit it. But psychologically, this doesn't even rate as a demon mindfuck."

Unable to help myself, I checked Drio's breathing. It was even, but slower than I would have liked.

"When Hybris fucked with Drio and you, Ro," I said, "she appeared as Asha and made you think his girlfriend, your cousin, had been alive and tortured all this time. Now that's psychological torture. Sorry."

Rohan shrugged it off. "You're not wrong."

"I'm missing something vital," I said. "Especially since there isn't even a wedding anymore. The Executioner has to know his compulsion has been broken, so how does he intend to spread the virus? If we move Drio and Isabella into quarantine, which can be done in seconds, no one else will be harmed. What's the demon's next move?"

Drio stirred in his sleep with a small whimper. The mass on his throat stretched tendrils out, crawling along his jawline and up his cheeks.

Nava sent her healing magic into him, but he didn't wake up. She let out a soft curse. "It's rooted in there deep. Leo, if you can't find the Executioner, or killing the demon doesn't destroy the virus, you have to—"

I glowered at her. "We quarantine them. And killing the Executioner *will* stop the virus. There is no Plan B. Do you understand?"

She nodded, her eyes bright with unshed tears.

Rohan dragged a chair in from the dining room up to the bed and sat down. "Find the demon."

I kissed Drio on the lips. "Hold on."

"Good luck. We'll take care of him." Nava hugged me.

I rode my Vespa to the offices of Dunn and Associates and walked in. Mozart's "Eine Kleine Nachtmusik" allegro flowed through the speakers and I sighed in relief. It meant Harry was in what passed for a good mood.

"You done with Mitra's case?" Harry stabbed at the keyboard with two fingers, his version of typing.

"I need the daeva's horn."

His bushy, bristly eyebrows shot up. "No."

"I wouldn't ask if it wasn't important."

He looked up at me. "The daeva is coming to retrieve her property tomorrow. I'm not going to risk payment or my neck by not having it."

"Drio is dying." I pressed my palms against my desk. It was the first time I'd let myself face the entire awful truth. "He has a demon virus inside him and if I can't find the demon behind it and kill him before the virus kills him in three days…"

Harry jabbed at a key. The Mozart cut out, replaced by the angry, crackling first movement of Brahms' First Symphony. "What? You planning on doing something stupid again? You don't even like him."

"Damn it, Harry. Enough, already. This isn't about being stupid, it's about doing whatever it takes to seize my shot at happiness. I'm finally with someone who challenges me to be the best version of myself, who sees me, *all* of me, and I'm not going to let it end here. If you're worried about the horn—"

Harry turned up the volume to near deafening levels.

"I won't let anything happen to me. I promise," I added off his glare.

Another minute of the stupid symphony screamed out of the speakers before Harry yanked open a drawer and tossed me the keys for the evidence cabinet. He turned down the music. "Boy Wonder better be worth it, or he'll answer to me."

I clutched them in my fist. "Thank you."

"Leonie." Harry pressed his lips together, a fierce expression on his face. "You get yourself killed and make me hand my business over to some stranger and I'll never forgive you."

I kissed his papery cheek. "I know."

He squeezed my hand. "Get out of here."

I hit up Derek Brown's place, an older bungalow up in Renfrew Heights, a middle class, fairly diverse neighborhood. It was raining and between the weather and the fact that it was already early evening and dark, there was no one to witness me skulking around Brown's property.

The only light on was in the living room at the front of the house. The curtains were wide open, his massive TV tuned to some overly bright sitcom.

I snuck around back and crept up his stairs, easily picking the lock on his door to slip into his kitchen that smelled of stale bacon fat and bro-dude. A number of stained pizza boxes were tossed on the counter and the sink was filled with mismatched glasses.

My boots snagged on a sticky patch as I silently crossed the room to check out the stack of mail tossed haphazardly on the counter. A couple of bills addressed to Derek and some junk flyers.

Brown lived alone, which would make this easier.

I glided down the short hallway and into the living room, careful to stay out of the glare of the TV so that neither my reflection nor my shadow would alert him to my presence.

Derek lounged in a brown recliner positioned in front of the TV, a beer in one hand. He wore a cheap white shirt that was baggy on his scrawny frame. Next to him was a folding TV table containing a cracked mirror with traces of what was probably cocaine, and a small none-too-clean knife.

I slipped behind the chair, put on a pair of protective gloves and extracted a pair of iron cuffs coated in a salt solution from a Ziplock bag that I'd taken from the evidence cabinet. The program cut to commercial, the volume automatically increasing. I darted out and slapped the cuffs on Derek.

Derek jumped to his feet. "Who the fuck are you?"

"Just want to have a little chat." I held up the daeva's horn and he stilled.

Diwrmachs were the werewolves of the demon world. Sort of. Hundreds of years ago, their line had been cursed by Nuckelavee, a Unique demon from Scotland's Northern Isles, who turned into a horse when on land. One of the diwrmachs mocked its form as weak, so Nuckelavee cursed the diwrmachs to turn into humans when the moon was full. Kind of an "I'll show you weak," baller move.

Living in the demon realm as they were, most of them were immediately slaughtered the first time they turned human. The rest fled, hiding on earth where at least they could blend in when the curse hit. For some reason, eating a daeva's horn staved off the curse for years at a time.

The demon sniffed the horn and his body rippled, his back twisting into a grotesque hump. Eating the horn held the curse at bay but being in its presence triggered his demon form. I had to get my answers and get out of here before he shifted.

"That's for real," he said.

"It is. Sit down and let's both get what we want."

He eased back into the recliner. "Which is?"

"Answers. You were dating Ally."

"The hell I was. That ala was batshit nuts. She tore me a new one when she found me with her sister." His torso bulged out with muscles like they were kernels of popcorn, while his neck, now bigger than my thigh, tore the elastic collar of his shirt.

"Imagine that. Who's her sister? Where do I find her?"

"Dead," he scoffed. "Some job in Italy a few days ago."

My pulse spiked. "Who hired her?"

"Gimme the horn." Brown's voice roughed, his arms thickening to three times their normal size. The cuffs strained and cracked off, hitting the nubby carpet.

I nailed him in the eyes with the salt and ghost pepper spray.

He ran a finger over his eyeball and sucked the mixture off. "Mmm. Spicy."

Pinning me in place with one enormous, meaty hand, he stole the horn and swallowed it, his neck muscles rippling as he gulped it down whole.

No horn, no real answers, and now I'd lost my bargaining chip. In P.I. speak, I was shit-out-of-luck.

Brown smacked his lips, and lunged, grabbing me around the waist and holding me bent over double.

I bit him, freeing myself, but the demon snagged my ankle and tugged. I hit the floor, clawing along the carpet as he dragged me to him.

My redcap raised her head and there wasn't even any blood. I dragged in a breath, but my lungs had seized up. Drio was dying, I was on the verge of becoming a monster, and if I didn't take control, all this was going to be moot because Brown would kill me.

My goblin's form grew in rapid-motion inside me.

Stop! *For Drio*. If I lost control to her, she'd attack this predator who was stronger and faster and it would be game over, for the daeva horn and Harry's faith in me. And more importantly for my chance to crack this mystery and save Drio. *Mate*.

If anything, the word "mate" wound her tighter. She snarled in frustration at me.

The diwrmach bit my boot, cracking a tooth on my reinforced steel toes. Blood dribbled out of the corner of his mouth. With a growl, he punched me in the gut.

I wheezed a pained gasp, the air driven from my lungs. The next punch clocked me in the head. The world swam in and out of focus.

Mate, my goblin said insistently.

The throbbing in my temples was fogging my brain and I couldn't figure out what she wanted from me.

The goblin nudged the bars of her cage.

Maybe it didn't have to be all or nothing with her? I lowered my guard a tiny amount. *Okay, then. Help me.* I braced myself, but she didn't take advantage, only infused a bit of her nature into me. A jagged need for violence rushed up through me, turning the world into shades of bloodlust red. For the first time ever, I embraced it.

I kicked over the TV table, infused with a burst of strength. Grabbing the knife, I slashed the diwrmach's tendons through his now-tattered, dingy white sports socks. His cries bounced off the walls, mixed in with canned laughter from the soundtrack and he collapsed on the ground, blood blossoming hot and coppery onto the carpet.

Before he could retaliate, I jammed the blade through his shoulder and into the underlay of the carpet. "Who hired the sister?"

The diwrmach pulled the knife out and tossed it away, rolling on top of me. Blood smeared on my skin and matted in my hair, spiking my adrenaline. I shoved him off me and jumped to my feet.

"Who?" When he didn't answer, I stomped on his stomach.

The demon grabbed my foot and threw me. I crashed into the edge of the coffee table. He rose up on his one good leg with a roar that turned to a wet gurgle, his eyes widening in surprise.

Gotcha, buddy. One more vital P.I. rule: no matter how gross, always, always have a back-up plan.

Ignoring the pain slashing through my right side, I dove behind the recliner as the Ipecac syrup that I'd liberally coated the horn in kicked in and he vomited all over the carpet.

I almost vomited too when I had to pluck the slimy horn out of demon bile and partially digested pepperoni pizza. Then I ran out the back door and into the night.

I pushed a strand of hair out of my face, a sticky line of blood hitting my cheek. The adrenaline was wearing off, leaving behind a deep and primal craving to feed. I could detoxify the salt and iron from the knife that was coated in the demon's blood and have a taste.

Je nourris. Tu nourris. Elle nourrit.

I put on my helmet with shaking hands and swung a leg over my Vespa.

The goblin was furious at me denying her sustenance after this fight. And also, deeply confused and betrayed by my actions. I battled her conflicted emotions as much as the blood cravings riding me.

The dark hid the worst of the stains on my clothing as I rode home, but the stench of blood still clung to me. The second I got inside my apartment, I raided my cupboard, eating a hunk of prosciutto until the protein kicked in and I felt more like myself.

My demon half was sulking but at the sight of Drio, still unconscious, she retreated.

"How'd it go?" Rohan hadn't moved from the foot of the bed. He blinked at my bloodied state, then carefully edged away from me.

"Got some answers. Need more," I said.

Stripping and throwing my clothes on my bathroom floor, I stepped under the scalding spray, eyes closed, letting the hot water sluice over me. The Executioner was whichever demon had hired Ally's sister. He or she had used her as a red herring to make us believe that this was a revenge plot. Well, it might still be a revenge plot, but if so, it had nothing to do with Ally, since the sister was dead, and trapping Drio had been a job for hire, rather than the sister's own initiative.

My gut told me that Drio was still integral to all this, while Isabella had unfortunately been a convenient pawn to help power the black mass, that virus intended to reach maximum potency and tear through the wedding guests like a weapon of mass destruction.

It was fiendishly clever to put us in the position of figuring out how to stop something magical when we couldn't use magic on the hosts because even healing magic made it stronger.

This demon was a master chess player, but I was the goddamn queen and it wasn't going to capture me. I had a king to protect at all costs.

I was so close to a breakthrough. I dumped a liberal handful of coconut body wash into my hands and scrubbed away every remaining trace of blood, racking my brain. *Beware the blood.* Anyone's blood? Drio and Isabella's? The Executioner's?

Once clean and dressed, with my stained clothes in the trash, I considered my next move. Nava had cleaned the horn and gone to return it to Harry. Nothing like demon pepperoni barf to show you your true friends.

"Hey, Ace." I cradled my phone between my shoulder as I pulled on my flat ankle boots.

"How are you doing?" Ari said. "Nava stopped by to fill us in."

Good. That would speed things up. "Would you shadow jump me to Antonia's place?" I quickly explained what I'd learned from Derek. "I need a tracker. See if there's any trace of the Executioner that would provide a clue to his identity."

"There in five."

Not only did Ari get here sooner, he brought Kane.

"I'm coming," Kane declared. "I may not have magic

anymore, but I have two working eyes and I track better than this one."

The nausea hit fast and hard when we landed on Antonia's property. I braced my hands on my thighs, swallowing down the taste of metallic bile. At least the property wasn't warded. I made a note to tell Antonia to remedy that. "I hate shadow transport."

"You'll get used to it eventually," Ari said.

"So you keep saying." I wiped my mouth with my hand.

I stayed with Kane in the woods that surrounded Antonia's house since the dense press of trees seemed like the more plausible place where the ala demon had hidden during her stay, and sent Ari off to check out the back gardens. The flat, cool dawn light was barely bright enough to track by, but by the time the sun was high in the sky, we'd done a thorough second sweep and hadn't found a thing.

It was already well into Saturday and provided Antonia was right, I only had until Monday to stop this.

"It was a long shot," I said. "Too much time has passed."

"Where do you want to go next?" Ari said.

My phone buzzed with a text from an unknown number. *One final game.*

It took a moment for my brain to make sense of the message, but when it did, an alarm rang in my mind, recent events rearranging to fall into place with a terrifying new clarity.

Drio was never the intended target after all.

I raised my head and sniffed. Copper and burnt amber. Oh God, I'd know that scent anywhere. I broke into a run, crashing through the woods in a blind panic, stumbling over roots, heedless of the thin, bare branches thwacking me about the face and shoulders.

Ari and Kane raced after me, yelling at me to stop.

I skidded into a small clearing and slid across the wet leaves.

Not wet with rain.

Wet with blood. My boot heel had snagged on a bloody red cap.

The guys pulled up short and Ari let out a low curse.

This was it. This was every nightmare I'd ever had, every monster lurking in every shadow. This was what I'd swore I'd banished, a life I'd left.

Except it wouldn't let me leave. How foolish had I been to have believed otherwise?

My chest stuttered and ice water crawled down my spine. "He's back."

"Who's back?" Kane demanded, shaking his gore-covered white shoes.

"My father."

15

Slow clapping was a demon invention. Not much of a claim to fame, but I was related to the demon who maybe pioneered it. What an inheritance.

Kobold sauntered toward me, his claps punctuating the air. Lanky in frame, he was no taller than I was, your garden variety green-skinned, pointy-eared, bearded male redcap with a perpetual scowl, dressed in rough, homespun cloth pants and shirt. He snatched up his red pointed hat from the forest floor and slapped it jauntily on his head. The hat was so soaked in blood that it glistened, but the blood was contained to the hat itself. Not a drop intruded into his straggly white hair. He didn't bother glamouring himself around me.

He'd placed some kind of bubble around us. Beyond it, Kane and Ari frantically searched for me, unable to see that I hadn't moved.

"The Executioner, I presume?" I sneered. "Bit of a lofty title for a low-ranking scum like yourself, Kobold."

"Show some respect to your da, child." His Scottish burr was a gruff rumble. He grabbed me and transported us.

The forest was gone; my friends were gone.

The crumbling ruins of a stone castle lay around me. Only

the listing wreckage of the turret was half-intact. Built on a tidal island, a sliver of grass as emerald as Drio's eyes surrounded the ruins, beyond which, a dark loch stretched to the horizon.

A cold salt-tinged wind rushed in off the water.

I tugged on the fat iron cuffs bolted to the wall that now encased my wrists. This was not the closure with my birth fiend that I'd had in mind. "Beware the blood? Might as well have said beware the bane of my existence. Should have known it was you."

Kobold leaned against the wall and widened his eyes theatrically. "Ah, but I'm not the Executioner."

I jerked against the cuffs. "Enough games."

"Life is a game, lassie. You win or you lose. But here's a free bit of strategy, a little gift straight from yer dear da: everyone ye love is doomed, all thanks to you."

"Meaning?"

Kobold shot me an enigmatic smile.

"You've forgotten one thing in your stupid games," I said.

"Wha's that, lass?"

"I'm the goddamn queen and I'm going to take you down."

"Och, Your Majesty." Bowing low, he tipped his hat at me then strolled out through the half-rotted wooden door frame.

He was lying about not being the Executioner. How else would he know about everyone being doomed? Kobold was a narcissist who constantly thought he was smarter than other people. Too bad for him, I had him figured out.

Besides, no one was doomed. Not if I got out of here and stopped the virus from breaking free.

By the time the sun was low in the sky, the purple shadows of dusk pressing in, my fingers and toes were numb from my exposure to the wind. My wrists were caked with red blisters, poisoned from rubbing against the iron cuffs.

My belly gurgled, empty and gnawing while my muscles spasmed. My thoughts spun, desperate and aware of the clock ticking. I needed more information, but I'd been calling him all day and the demon hadn't condescended to return.

When he finally did, he'd fed, his cap newly replenished with hot, rich blood.

My goblin self snapped her eyes open. I banished her back to her dark hole, but she didn't listen. She was aware of the threat Kobold presented and held back due to some primal instinct about our sire, or maybe just remembering the scar he'd given me on our last daddy-daughter date.

"Why did you do it?" I asked Kobold. It came out as a cracked half-sob. I swallowed to get saliva into my mouth.

"Do ye ken the shame you heaped on me?" He grabbed my chin, his calloused fingers digging into my flesh. "You chose our mortal enemies."

"I told you I was human years ago."

"You're not listening, lassie. Witches. Rasha. You debased my legacy and chose them. Then you tried to have Gog and Magog take the magic I'd given you. Throw it out like garbage, when you should have prostrated yourself before me in thanks for raising you above your weak, human side. My clan has issued a leadership challenge unless I bring my successor into the fold. It's time you took your place, even if ye must overcome yer human filth." He let go with a violent shove. "I won't have you make a mockery of my legacy."

"I don't want your legacy. And I'm not your successor but I'm not weak either. You'll see. I didn't set that virus loose but I will be the one to stop it."

He shot me an indulgent—and patronizing—look.

"Ye wound me, but if I must give up on my one and only heir, then at least convince me that my blood doesn't run strong in your veins." He whipped off his hat and I recoiled at the fat, beady-eyed rat sitting on his head. He snapped her neck, hanging the carcass on a hook protruding from the stones next to me. "For every sip of blood ye take from her, I'll answer a question."

I remained silent, my eyes trained on the half-wall across the room mottled with moss and not at the trickle of blood staining the rat's fur. I tried to seal my nostrils so I couldn't smell the tantalizing aroma of fresh blood.

"Call when you get hungry." He left.

Think, Leo. While I still could.

This was Kobold's revenge, but it was against me, not Drio. Drio was as much a pawn as Isabella. I ignored the rumbling in my stomach and my brain's commands to just lean sideways. Just a little bit.

Build a timeline, kiddo. I clung to Harry's voice, calling up every rule he'd ever taught me to save me now.

The showdown in Jerusalem had set Kobold off. My public affinity with the witches and Rasha. That was when? Around September 16? He got mad and decided on one last game to force my goblin nature. It always came back to that.

No judgement until all the facts are in.

But it was a fact. The one irrefutable fact of every single visit I'd suffered with Kobold. He wanted my demon side to reign.

She growled her agreement with that idea.

How? By getting Nava engaged to Drio?

Kobold had been stalking me for most of my life. Other people got goosebumps when someone walked over their grave, I got them when I sensed his eyes on me. He'd have known about my friendship with Nava, and if he'd watched the livestream of what had happened in the plaza by the Wailing Wall, he'd have seen Drio stop me from touching Gog and Magog. Was that enough to put Drio on Kobold's radar? No, that wouldn't be enough for the psychotic fuck. It would have to be something more knife-twisting.

Did he know, even then, that Drio was special? Was shacking up my lover with my best friend Kobold's way of showing me that all humans would turn on me? If so, there was the psychological torture I'd been missing.

Which brought me back to Nava and her sense she was

being watched the night of Rohan's performance. Kobold had likely been there, but once he'd seen her with Rohan, he'd known he couldn't use her. Enter Isabella, the smart, kind, Italian witch who had everything I didn't: scads of magic, no dark side to combat, and the guy I'd risked everything for.

Between the wind lashing me to a dangerous numbness and the clawing hunger, it was getting harder to think. I eyed the rat: cold, stiff, and soaked with congealed blood. Part of me was repulsed, the other part drooled like the damn thing was a three-star Michelin entrée.

I ordered my goblin to stand down and remember Drio. My only way out of this was via my wits and for that, I needed my logical side in control.

As far as I was concerned, the universe had dealt me a shitty hand with the sperm donor. I'd lived my life shrouded in secrets, at times clinging to my humanity with sheer grit and a smile on my face, but cling to it I had, no matter what, and I wasn't going to lose it now.

I closed my eyes, practicing a breathing and meditation routine to feel more centered. By the time the shakiness had left me, the moon had streaked a bright arc across the night sky, then given way to weak sunlight.

No wind today. It wasn't much of a blessing. The sun warmed me enough to get feeling back in my body, and with it came the blaze of pins and needles in my arms and legs from being chained up. My shoulder muscles were strained from my weight placement with the position of the cuffs.

My heart beat faster at the thought of every second slipping away, but it was a new day with new hope.

"Knock. Knock." Kobold entered holding a raw hunk of beef, dripping blood.

My mouth watered and my goblin flexed her claws. I could feel their deadly sharp pricks inside my body.

He kicked the rat out over one of the collapsed walls toward the water, waving the fresh meat in front of me. "One little lick?"

"You're getting soft in your old age if you think Drio getting married was going to make me go goblin." Half my words were mumbled slurs, but Kobold got the gist.

"Got that did you? You always were a clever girl, Leonie." The bastard sounded proud, like he was personally responsible for my intelligence. "You deserve a reward."

He swiped a finger along the beef, coating the tip in blood, and attempted to press it to my lips.

My lips had opened partway before I caught myself and clamped them together, thrashing my head, fighting him and my redcap who clamored for the blood.

"Hold still, child. Stop fighting your nature." He grabbed my chin again and rubbed the blood against my lips.

I whimpered, my fortress of humanity starting to crumble. I tried to wipe the blood off on my jacket sleeve, but Kobold held me still until it had dried on my lips, the salty tang of the sea and the smell of my own sweat buried beneath that rich copper aroma.

He tossed the meat at my feet with a splat, half-on my boots. I kicked it off onto the dirty floor, but my boots were smeared.

"Yer old man was having a wee bit of fun with the engagement. Rile you up before the final game began."

Je nourris. Tu nourris. Elle nourrit.

"Leonie."

I snapped my attention back to him, my breathing coming in harsh pants. I'd licked my bottom lip clean.

Kobold's eyes gleamed in triumph and my goblin demanded more. I had no food to force her back into submission, only sheer will power and the lure of our mate that needed saving and I used every iota of both to remain in control.

"The virus," I said. "How many gems did it cost you?"

"A lot, but it was worth every last tiny jewel to make you pay for dishonoring me."

"And the ala demon?"

"Eh. Help is cheap." He peered into my eyes and grunted in satisfaction. "You can't win this one, my girl. Might as well feed." When I didn't respond, he shook his head and exited.

I tasted metal on my tongue because I'd sucked all the cow's blood off my lips. I threw my head back and screamed.

Spent, I sagged against my cuffs, my head drooping forward. I'd been here a day and a half and I wasn't sure how much longer I could last. The universe took mercy on me and exhaustion claimed me.

Leo. Harry's voice in my head was urgent. *The wedding wasn't the final game.*

"I can't, Harry."

Then everyone you care about dies. Get your shit together.

I struggled to see. The world had been reduced to slits viewed through burning eyes. Too much iron exposure.

Dawn was breaking, a beautiful canvas of pink and gold. I tried to care, but the only thing that interested me was the congealed blood on that raw meat.

My goblin snickered and reality re-asserted itself. Today was Monday. One final day, one last shot to get out of here.

I wasn't going to fail. I jolted upright because I'd been straining as far forward as possible to get to the beef.

"Help." It was a soundless cry.

Asking the universe for help was like making a wish with a genie. You might get what you want but not in the way you'd intended.

Freezing rain sluiced down over me. I turned my cracked, swollen lips upwards, desperate for water and drank until my thirst was slaked and my throat was no longer glued together. I was drenched and shivering uncontrollably, my teeth chattering hard enough to break, but the soaking had brought me back to my senses.

I tangled my stiff fingers into my hair and pulled as hard as I could, relishing the pain. The bite cut through the rest of my haze. With fumbling movements, I traced my eyes, my nose, my lips. Reaffirming that I was human, each touch holding my monster at bay.

No food, no freedom, no assistance. I doubled down on my weak focus.

The virus. My hunch on that score had been correct. If anyone could procure something like that, it was Kobold. When I was little, he'd shown me rare jewels that mankind had written off as lost forever. He could easily have brought the diamond to a demon capable of creating and implanting the virus. That same demon would have compelled the ring and iron bar, because if Kobold had that ability, he'd have compelled me years ago.

I had no opportunity to get to the demon who'd created the virus before it was too late for Drio and Isabella, which meant I had to stop it another way.

Kobold had been keeping tabs on me and known I'd snapped the compulsion, yet this game wasn't over, because he hadn't achieved his end goal.

He hadn't unleashed my goblin side.

Soon, she whispered. *My time will come.*

This imprisonment wasn't Kobold's bold move. He could have kidnapped me at any time, but he'd gone to all this trouble with the engagement and the virus. He had one more play, so what was it? If I'd remained free, what could possibly have broken me to the point where my demon could get her claws in me and take over for good?

I'd have to wrong someone I cared about in the most horrible way. Violate my moral code on a fundamental level.

My breath hitched as the answer dropped into my brain with a shocking clarity. He'd said he wasn't the Executioner.

I was the Executioner.

"Kobold!!!!" My scream tore from my throat, bouncing off the ruins before floating up into the sky.

He appeared instantly, holding a pint glass full of fresh blood. "You called?"

"The fail-safe. You were counting on me to break the compulsion and destroy the ring so that the virus would jump directly into Drio and Isabella."

"I've watched you all these years. Smart, deadly. You'd make a fine heir. I had no doubt you'd figure it all out and play into my hands."

"How? That doesn't make me the Executioner. Drio and Isabella were doomed the moment you put that virus in the ring. All of it is your doing, not mine." I bit the inside of my cheek to keep my voice steady. "They'll be quarantined by now. And if you think you can use my blood to release the virus somehow—"

"Don't need your blood, lass." He swirled the blood around in the pint glass and I followed the motion, mesmerized, cravings wracking my body. "Soon as the virus was activated inside those two, it infected everyone who came into contact with them. And so on and so forth. It's winging its way through the magic community by now. That *is* your doing."

I swallowed my gasp at the danger I'd unknowingly put my friends in, but I wasn't about to give Kobold a weakness to hold over me and outwardly I shrugged. "Then we all die and you still don't get what you want."

"You won't die. You're immune. See how useful it is to be a goblin? Small wonder most halflings choose that part of themselves and not the weak human side."

"I'll die from hunger and cold then, because I *will* die before I let her free. I live as a human and I'll die as one." Still soaked through, my tongue barely worked anymore and my skin had turned blue, my joints stiff.

I kicked the meat still laying at my feet away from me. It was a feeble kick and the meat didn't really go anywhere, but it was the symbolism that mattered. "You won't win."

He patted my cheek. "You've risked everything outing yourself to those people. That means that those witches and Rasha are important to you."

"More of us, less of you," I spat.

"Exactly. If they die, who is going to protect all those fragile humans?" He took off his cap and scratched his hair with a gnarled, blood-stained finger. "I'm going to offer you one last choice, because you're my only child and I'm feeling sentimental. I'll give you the antidote." He set down the pint glass and removed a vial of blood from his pockets.

"Another trick."

"No tricks. This is the antidote."

Blood to feed the virus and blood to kill it? Whose blood? Was this also something to beware of?

"It's fast-acting," he said. "Give it to one of the witches and they'll have everyone right as rain in seconds. All you have to do is choose. The lives of all those magic people, the protectors of humanity, in exchange for one single life."

Shock slammed into me, hot and fierce.

"No." I fought against the cuffs. "I won't kill him."

"If you truly prize your humanity, you'll choose the greater good. Your emotions will be your undoing, girl. Always is with humans. He's going to die anyway. End it. Kiss him farewell and send him into the gentle night. Feeding off your beloved. How romantic."

"You're insane."

Kobold chuckled, the sound skating up my spine. "Now that I think about it, this isn't really a fair choice. *All* of you should have a voice."

"I swear I'll kill you."

"You swore to do that years ago, and yet here I stand."

And then I'll feed. My goblin cackled like a hyena.

Drio. Nava. Harry. Ari. Rohan. Kane. My mom. Madison. I fixed the images of every single person that meant anything to me firmly in my mind's eye.

Kobold picked up the glass of blood, grabbed my hair and tipped my head back. "You have twenty minutes before the virus kills them all. Tick tock." He poured the entire contents of the pint glass over my mouth.

Resistance was futile. I opened wide and with a "Please, sir, may I have another?" my goblin roared forward, my dark nature surging into the forefront of my consciousness as I drank the blood down, hot and thick and delicious.

It was heady. I didn't change forms, didn't have any body other than my weak human one but it had finally transcended its pathetic nature. The world blazed with new and glorious colors. I tracked an eagle's nest hidden in a tree that was miles off, hearing her cries like she was here beside me.

My exhaustion, my dehydration, it all fell away. The iron cuffs burned worse, but it was a mild price to pay. Why had I ever fought this?

My puny human side tried to show me faces of people as if they mattered. Humans were a dime a dozen. I grabbed the pint glass, shaking it to get every last drop.

"Good girl," Kobold said. "I told you your true nature would win out, Leonie, and I was right. The world will be ours for our taking. Humans will fear you."

A shudder of disgust kicked through me and I snapped out of my demon haze, mentally punching my goblin in the head, and seizing a semblance of control. I didn't want the world. Not like that. Not like a nightmare.

But was there any waking up from this one?

If I didn't save the many, didn't choose the greater good, I'd be wreaking the same level of destruction on the world as if I did nothing.

If I didn't save Drio, I'd be wreaking destruction on my heart.

Drio had trusted me with *his* heart and now I was supposed to eat it? Really rocking this girlfriend gig. I stifled a half-hysterical laugh.

Save the many or kill the one?

I was a murderer either way. Either way, my soul was dead.

The arguments chased themselves through my fuzzy brain while my redcap chanted her preference. I ignored the smacking sounds in my head and the taste of blood on my tongue as she forced me to lick my face clean, keeping a tight hold on my sanity.

I had no weapons and even if I got out of the cuffs, I was in no condition to take Kobold on my own. Even rested and at full strength, I was no match for him.

Could I slow Drio's heart down just enough to trick Kobold into thinking he was dead? No, I doubted Kobold could be fooled. He dealt in death. Any perceived betrayal and he'd destroy the antidote.

Save the many or kill the one?

Win as much as I could in this rigged game, or lose Drio? Either way, I became the Executioner.

Either way, my mind would snap, my goblin side would take control, and Kobold would win.

Think, Leo.

With ten minutes left before the virus killed everyone, I gave him my answer.

"Drio. I'll kill him." Tiny drops of ice like pearls rolled down my cheeks.

Kobold unlocked the cuffs with a rusty chuckle. "What a fucking bam. Second girlfriend he's losing to a demon."

The instant the cuffs were off, my legs buckled out from under me and I hit the stone floor on my knees. The thwack was so loud that I was sure I broke something, but there was no pain.

That would come later.

Je nourris. Tu nourris. Elle nourrit. Feed. Feed. Feeeeeeed! My goblin was worse than a demented child on a sugar high.

Kobold scooped me up and portalled us into a sealed room.

Isabella and Drio were asleep on twin beds, hooked to IVs. Every inch of their exposed skin was covered in the shifting black mass. A faint sound of wind accompanied the shapes' movement. It was beautiful.

Horrible.

Just like me.

My inner demon clapped her hands at what was to come. One more taste of blood and she'd snap free and take over forever.

Kobold eyed Isabella. "Och, dessert."

"Don't touch her," I said.

"Leo!" Nava's gasp came over a loudspeaker. She didn't realize it was pointless being on the other side of this door. The damage was done.

I pushed out of Kobold's grasp, preferring to be sprawled on the floor in a heap than depend on him. "Keep out, Nava. I mean it. Just… one minute and you'll have the antidote."

"Aye," the demon agreed. "So long as Leonie here comes through."

I half-crawled to Drio's bed. "Put the antidote to the right of the door."

I didn't trust Kobold in the slightest that he'd just hand it over. There was always another bit of mindfuckery where Daddy Dearest was concerned.

Rolling his eyes, he set the vial where I'd instructed.

I motioned for him to move away and he shuffled to the foot of the beds.

"Gonna wake him up," I said.

Kobold shrugged. "Five minutes. Use it as you see fit."

I tore the IV free from Drio's hand and, with my magic, pulled out the drugs they'd been feeding him to ease his pain. His eyes fluttered open. Those beautiful emeralds that saw everything around him with innate clarity, the light, the dark, and those of us trapped between.

"Leonie. Bella." He blinked into alertness, his eyes narrowing at my appearance.

"Doesn't matter," I whispered.

His gaze flicked to Kobold. "Did we move up family dinner?"

I laughed, my still-swollen eyes pooling with tears and, worming my hand under his shirt, placed it directly over his heart. His body tightened under my palm as I drew blood, the drops welling to the surface and smearing against my skin.

His breath caught, but he met my eyes, and relaxed against my touch.

My heart broke, but there was only one way forward. I brushed my lips over his and whispered what was in my heart directly into his ear.

"Now!" I snarled and licked my hand. "Blood!"

My goblin tore free.

The world turned red, my dirty human finally put in her place. I was as I was meant to be.

The Rasha whose yummy blood I consumed rose from his bed and flashed to my father.

I started for my father's side but…

Mate.

The Rasha nailed my father in his kill spot. He gave a gasp and disappeared.

I howled and lunged for the hunter.

Two more burst through the door. I scoured my human memories. Nava and Rohan. They'd meant something to the human. They meant nothing to me.

A malevolent smile curled across my face. Witches and Rasha. I would feed well.

16

The witch blasted me back against the wall.

I cracked my head. Like that would stop me. Grinning at her, I ran my fingers through the blood on the back of my skull and deliberately licked them off. "Thanks for the snack."

The Rohan Rasha swore. He supported the blond Rasha, the one that I'd fed from. The one I had to protect?

No. He'd killed Kobold. We were enemies. I knew the blond one's taste now. *The weight of his bottom lip, the slide of his olive skin, his hot fullness pushing inside me, and that deep voice edged with laughter and danger saying "Cuore mio."*

My heart.

I blinked. Shook my head.

"The antidote. It's a dud. Food coloring in liquid glycerin." The Rohan Rasha held up the vial that he'd dipped a finger into, frowning at the shadows shifting and churning under the blond one's skin.

Laughing, I ran at the witch.

Frowning, she looked between me and the antidote. "Leo, you did it."

Those were the last things I heard before her magic engulfed me and I blacked out.

I came to with a jackhammer of a headache in one of the beds in the quarantine room, wearing my softest pair of leggings and an oversized sweater. My goblin had retreated.

Drio sprawled in a chair next to the bed.

My heart stuttered at the sight of him. "I didn't eat you?"

He gave me a filthy grin that sent sparks ping-ponging deep inside me. "Not yet."

I sat up.

"Wait." He crossed his arms. "How do I know it's really you and not goblinissima?"

I punched him. "Are you fucking kidding me? Too soon, buddy. I am so going to stab—"

Drio took hold of me, careful of the blisters still circling my wrists, and pulled me to him, hugging me like I was the most precious thing in the world.

I grabbed him back just as tightly. Alive. We were alive and nothing else mattered.

"Visitors!" Nava sang, the door to the quarantine room crashing open.

"Seriously, I want one of him." Isabella bounced on her toes.

Antonia scolded her in Italian.

Drio groaned and pushed my hair back from my face, holding my gaze with his own a moment before releasing me. "Later."

I shivered at the dark promise in his voice.

"For sure." I curled my fingers into the blanket, flashes of myself having gone super-demony assaulting me. I had no regrets for what I'd done, wouldn't apologize for what I was, but I braced myself for a new battle of acceptance. "Everyone hale and whole?"

Antonia rushed me. I pulled the blankets up like that could ward her off, gasping when she too, crushed me in a hug. Geez, what was with the Italians today?

"You want biscotti?" she said and handed me a container heaping with raisin ones. "I make them for you. Any time."

I licked my lips, Biscotti, maybe not. However… I sent my boyfriend a sly glance. "Will you make me cornetti? The cream ones?"

Drio snorted.

"Please don't mind him." I elbowed the Rasha in question. "He's just jealous because raisin biscotti are his favorites."

Drio shot me a look of betrayal so absolute I almost couldn't keep a straight face as Antonia beamed and pinched my cheeks.

"Sì. Whenever you want. Ah, bellissima."

"That's it," Isabella said. "You'll be expected at family dinner now."

"That sounds perfect," I said, imagining a future bursting with delicious confections and Antonia perpetually haranguing my boyfriend. "You're okay?"

"I'm fine." She beamed at me. "Ari even told me I wouldn't have to wait until they'd secured a facility to start training. He's hooked me up with this amazing hunter, Danilo."

Well, Danilo was a great Rasha. He was also into witches. Maybe Isabella's wish for another shot at a Rasha wasn't that far off from coming true.

Nava's shoulders were shaking. She jerked her chin at Antonia and mimed slashing her throat. Ha. Ari was evil. Antonia would crucify Danilo if he so much as touched Isabella.

Antonia and Isabella stayed for a few more moments before announcing they'd let me rest. "I'll send the cornetti over, pronto," Antonia said, on her way out the door.

I smirked at Drio.

He gave me a long-suffering sigh, then sat down next to me, pulling me into his side.

Nava rolled her eyes and squished onto the bed on my other side. "I predate you," she told him. She sent her healing magic into me, then satisfied, leaned against me.

I prodded the bandage wrapped around my head. "You almost broke my skull, lady."

"You tried to kill me," she said.

"You tried to kill me first. Weeks ago at Hex Factor HQ."

Nava snickered. "True. Now we're even."

"Not really. You way outpower me."

"Hey, I didn't expect you to pack such a punch as a goblin. But yes, alas, I am still stronger." She kissed each of her fists. "You will never get the jump on me because I am exponentially more kick-ass."

"Hardly exponential," I said.

"Exponential infinity."

"Madonna mia, how does Rohan put up with the two of you?" Drio said.

"We're delightful," Nava said.

"Delightful infinity." I threw my arms around these two people that meant everything to me. "You're all okay? You figured out what I was trying to tell you about the antidote?"

Nava intertwined her fingers and stretched out her hands. "It was obvious. Since you let your goblin side out, which is not a typical Monday for you, combined with your lusty cry of 'blood,' it must have been your goblin blood that had the antibodies needed to kill the virus."

"It wasn't obvious at all," Drio said, in a snarky voice.

Nava and I grinned at each other. It had always driven Ari nuts when we were growing up how Nee and I could speak in total shorthand and understand each other. It was all well and good when the two of them did it, but I think he got peeved since I wasn't her twin.

But sheesh, had it come in handy now.

"You are surrounded by women of genius," Nava said. "Deal with it."

"Yeah, well, geniuses, we're all just lucky the antidote got distributed in time, because it came down to the wire."

"How close to the wire are we talking?" I said.

"Too close." Drio played with my hair, massaging my scalp with his strong fingers. "It helped that it worked like the virus itself and spread rapidly. Nava cured Antonia and Isabella, then they fanned out to other witches and so on."

"Kane and Ari?"

"All good," Nava said. "Other than Kane's theatrics that he had PTSD from your kidnapping."

"Excellent. My brilliant plan worked. You may anoint me with gratitude."

"I still cannot believe your idea of deathbed endearments was to whisper Kobold's kill spot." Drio scowled at me. So much for gratitude.

"Like you weren't totally turned on by that," Nava scoffed.

"Was I supposed to tell you how much I cared about you?" I said. "It wasn't the time or the place for that."

"Deathbed," Drio said. "The definition of 'time and place.'"

"My version was much more romantic," I said. "'Right collarbone. Up and at 'em, hunter. I'll make it worth your while.'"

"That last part was okay," he admitted.

"You suck at gratitude," I said.

Drio gave me a look hot enough to smolder the blankets.

"Ew." Nava scrunched up her face.

"Rohan, call your girlfriend," Drio said.

"I'm not a dog," Nava replied.

"Sparky, stop torturing Drio and give them a moment." Rohan's voice came over the loudspeaker.

Nava raised her eyebrows. "You want me to leave?"

"Yes. But I love you." I gave her my most adorable smile. "Schmugs."

"Hmph. I'm only schmugging back because I am the superior friend." She slid off the bed and left.

Drio gently pushed me down to the mattress, propped on his elbow above me. "Kobold had you for two and a half days." Every word was granite hard. "You had blood on your face, which means that was the only food you'd gotten and even battered and bruised, you still showed up fighting for what was right." He stroked my cheek. "You still had the strength of mind to trick him. You were spectacular."

I warmed under his praise. "That's what I'm talking about."

"How did you know the antidote was a dud?"

"Years of dealing with Kobold. He hadn't created the virus, so killing him wasn't going to destroy squat, but he'd mentioned I was immune. When I saw the vial, I drew my conclusions. Sorry about bleeding you. I hope it didn't hurt too much."

"I hope killing your father didn't hurt too much." His voice was light, but he watched me warily.

"You killed Harry?" I clapped my hand over my mouth.

"No jokes. It must bother you." The corners of Drio's eyes were pulled tight, his lips clamped together in a line.

"You said it yourself. You rid the world of evil, and I will never see you as anything other than good and noble for doing that."

Drio didn't look convinced so I pulled my sweater up, twisting to show him the faint scar on my stomach. "Want to know how I got this? It wasn't on a case. Kobold gave it to me when I was fifteen."

Drio's eyes turned to flint, but he shook his head. "Still—"

"No. He wasn't worth any more energy. You killed a demon who was literally the stuff of my nightmares, and I'm glad he's dead." I traced the scar. "His shadow has hung over me my entire life. Part of me has lived in fear, waiting for our next encounter. Well, it's finally over. I'm free."

The game had been played, the chessboard littered with pieces, but the king and queen were still standing.

"Then I'm glad to be of service." He captured my mouth and I wrapped my arms around him like a lifeline, the bruising kiss raw and hard, leaving me arching against him, breathless.

"Ahem."

"Go away, Nee." I barely moved my lips off Drio's.

"Get a room. Unless we're about to have a very interesting double date."

"Jesus," Rohan muttered from the doorway where the two of them stood. "What is it with you? Hey, Leo. Thanks for saving us."

"No prob. FYI, your girlfriend has been trying to get in my pants for ages."

Nava planted her hands on her hips. "I'm just saying. We're all young, good-looking, sexual beings."

"Not gonna happen," Ro and Drio said.

"Then go home," she said, "because Drio is a surly bastard when all is not right with you and I don't want to deal with him until he gets laid and is nice again. As nice as he gets," she amended.

Drio gave her his Torture Time smile.

Life was back to normal and it was grand.

I WAS quiet in the cab ride back to my place. When we got inside my apartment, I flicked on the lights, drenching us in a honey-warm glow. I sat down cross-legged on the sofa, patting it for Drio to join me. My black knit blanket was still tossed on the cushions, so I folded it, silver star facing out.

"What's up?"

"All these years," I said. "I've thought of myself as two distinct halves. Even if I could, I'll never again try to give up my goblin side. Those shadows allowed me to go as dark as I had to in order to fight the good fight. Hell, they fueled the good fight. But I'm not doing this anymore. I can't keep fighting her. I don't want to keep fighting her."

"Meaning?"

I took his hand. "I'm going to invite her out, let us finally be one and at peace. If it doesn't freak you out too much, I'd like you to be here."

What I didn't say was that if anything went wrong, he had to take care of it.

"I'm beside you every step of the way," he said.

Still holding his hand, I closed my eyes, imagining the white light that I'd always protected myself from her with forming into a door that I opened. She was wary of the gesture. Our history of fighting for dominance made her believe this was a trick.

No. Come out. Please.

My goblin was like a cat in an unfamiliar place. Skittish and tentative, her claws unsheathed and ready to slash. She sensed Drio and paused.

I remained still, letting his scent envelop her. She did recognize him as mate, but he was also the one who'd killed Kobold and she recognized his power.

Drio gave a soft huffing sound and I opened my eyes.

I'd burrowed my head into the crook of his neck, forcing him back against the cushions.

"Whoops." I detangled myself.

"You okay?"

"Yeah." I closed my eyes again, focused on sending her encouraging thoughts. Whenever her form had previously taken shape, it had existed as a hard outline against the white light. Black and white.

It was time to become gray.

I let the two colors, the two sides of myself blend and swirl, until they settled into a soft charcoal color that pulsed through me stretching up to the crown of my head, jutting out to my fingertips, and down to the ends of my toes. I didn't lose any sense of myself. In fact, a deep tension left my body.

I'd fought her for so long, but she wasn't my enemy. Was I going to have to still take measures to curb her bloodlust? Sure, but my human side would eat French fries 24/7 if I could get away with it. She gave me enhanced hearing, the ability to detoxify, and magic to kill demons. In short, a lot of really cool and useful qualities.

Being one with her was comforting. Like a blanket.

Frowning, I opened my eyes.

"How do you feel?" Drio asked. "You don't look any different."

"Did you know that I started knitting when I was about six?" I leapt off the couch and went into my bedroom, throwing open my closet. Inside was a floor-to-ceiling shelving unit filled with dozens of handmade blankets.

"Whoa," Drio said.

"Our teacher taught us to knit for an art project and I never stopped. These aren't even all the ones I've ever made. I gave most of them away."

"That's great, bella, but I don't understand what it has to do with your goblin."

"Six was around the age that Kobold started visiting me. She and I didn't used to be separate. I think I forced her aside when he started coming around. Without properly understanding why or even what I was doing, I tried to rid myself of anything that was like Kobold, but I messed up. She never intended to hurt me because she was me. Yes, she was a demon, but I made her into a monster." I shook my head. "I made part of *myself* into a monster. You asked me how I felt? I feel like there's a warm, comfy blanket inside me when for years all there's been is barbed wire."

He wrapped his arms around me. "I'm glad you're finally fully yourself."

"Me too." I looked up at him. "But there's one more thing I need to do. Will you wait for me for about an hour?"

"Of course."

17

Schubert's piano sonata in A minor streamed over the speakers. Harry was at maximum anxiety levels.

"Leonie Hendricks, that poor daeva horn was covered in—oomph!" Harry grunted as I threw my arms around him.

"I'm sorry I made you worry."

He wrapped his arms tightly around me. "You going to stop taking years off my life, now?"

"Yes. You can paint to your heart's content. But no more freaky kittens." I stepped back. "Kobold's dead."

"Good riddance."

"And I've stopped fighting my demon side."

He raised an eyebrow. "About time."

A pang of sadness speared my chest at the thought of Harry retiring, but he was excited for this next chapter of his life. Like I was. "The business will be fine."

"Not for another couple of years because it's not quite ready for me to leave it yet, but it will be." He glanced out the front window. "Who's that coming–? Oh no. No. Not today." He bolted up from his seat. "I was finally facing a moment's peace and now she's going to come in here and spew all that brimfire nonsense."

I clamped down on his wrist. "Don't you dare leave. I can't face her alone."

"Let your demon do it."

"I am my demon. That's why I called her." I steeled myself. "I'm going to tell her."

"This is a very bad idea," he said, but he sat back down.

"I don't want to live a lie from my own mother."

The bell over the front door jingled.

"Leonie." My mom hurried over to kiss me. Her nylon dress with the small floral pattern rubbed against my arms and her liberal dose of rose perfume wafted around us.

Harry pointedly fanned the air.

My mother opened the purse she had slung over her arm. "I know you said you had something important to tell me, sweetie, but first, let me give you this."

She removed a gold crucifix on a chain from a blue box. "You have some rough customers in your line of work. Who knows how many of them are demons in disguise?" She crossed herself, glaring at Harry. All of mom's P.I. knowledge was based off what she saw on TV, and she was convinced that every shift involved a gun battle and a high-speed chase. I had a sneaking suspicion that Magnum P.I. and 1940s detective movies had also influenced her thinking because past Christmas gifts had included both a Hawaiian shirt and a trench coat.

Ooh, with Drio around, that coat might come in handy.

"This is a great idea," Harry muttered.

I was about to elbow him, but then I took a good look at my mother.

Mom looked older than her forty-three years. She'd spent a long time being bitter over the "man" who'd knocked her up and left her, and the existence of demons had only confirmed that other than me, her pride and joy, life was shit and full of bad things. In the wake of all that, she'd joined a church, well, several, but she was happier for it.

And now I was about to tell her that the little girl she'd

watched *Roman Holiday* with and laughed over popcorn with was a demon all along? There was being honest and there was being kind, and looking at my mother, this wouldn't be kind. I'd made peace with my goblin, I could make peace with the fact that my mother would never truly know all of me, because she wouldn't be able to accept it.

She'd accepted my bisexuality without issue. That would have to be enough.

I took the crucifix. "Thanks for the cross, Mom. And don't worry, this world just got a lot less dangerous."

She gave me a puzzled smile. "That's nice, sweetie. What was so important that I had to rush over from my church social?"

"I'm seeing this really great guy and I was wondering if you and Harry would like to come for dinner with us tomorrow night."

Harry did a double-take, then grunted. "Been meaning to size him up."

I rolled my eyes. "Mom. How about you?"

"I'd love to. Ooh, I know the perfect place to take you all. The restaurant at Queen Elizabeth Park. You always did love those gardens. We can go for a walk beforehand."

"That would be great," I said.

Harry snorted, but only half-sarcastically. Good enough for me.

"Honey, I'm home."

Drio came out of my bedroom. "How'd it go?"

"Well, I didn't tell my mother that I'm a demon, we're both going to dinner tomorrow with her and Harry so you can be put through an inquisition, and she gave me this." I tossed the crucifix on the coffee table.

"She knows it's demons, not movie vampires, right?"

"I vant to suck your blood." I mock-jumped him, arms

outstretched. "But no, I think she figures it's all the same. At least that's over."

"And it's just the two of us."

The tension rushed in to fill the space between us, thrumming so hard it was almost palpable. I squirmed, my clit throbbing. My nipples hardened in anticipation, my entire body flushed.

Our gazes snagged, so loaded that desire shimmered like heat between us.

"Hey, hunter?" I placed his hand on my heart. "Cuore mio. That's what I really wanted to whisper to you. Because you are. Always and forever." I sucked on my bottom lip. "Now, fuck me."

He laughed. "Who said romance is dead?" His hands tightened on my hips and I winced. "You're still injured."

"My body, my call."

Drio planted an open-mouthed kiss on me that was zero-to-a-billion dirty. He let out an erotic growl, his tongue tangling with mine and I ground up against him. The kiss went from devouring to tender and back into holy-fuck territory. My entire body was on fire. This kiss was going to ruin me and I luxuriated in it. I fell, deeply, permanently, trusting in him to catch me.

He hauled me up around his hips, pinning me against him, and walked us into the bedroom.

"Sofa. Closer," I gasped.

"Not enough room," he purred and lay me on the mattress. "Nemmeno immagini cosa ho intenzione di farti. You have no idea what I'm going to do to you."

He bunched my sweater in his hands, inching it up my sides, his calloused palms dragging along my skin. He pulled the sweater free, his eyes roaming my body in lust and fascination.

I cupped one breast, teasing my nipple.

His breathing grew harsh and he ripped off my leggings. He nudged my legs open. "Fatti penetrare."

My legs fell open. I leaned back on my elbows, my eyes rapt on him, holding my breath at what he'd do first.

"Hmm." He traced my nipple that jumped to attention under his touch. "No." He dipped his tongue into my navel, nipping at my belly.

I giggled.

He raised his head, a predatory expression on his face, his eyes burning emeralds. "You're laughing, bella? Perhaps I am doing this wrong?"

His accent got stronger the more aroused he got. It was more pronounced than I'd ever heard it, flowing over me like rich whiskey.

"Perhaps you are," I said.

He grinned at me and the butterflies in my stomach dipped and swooped. "A challenge?" He swiped his finger along my clit, slow, long teases that shivered through me. "Come sei bagnata. You're so wet."

"Yes," I breathed.

"Amo il tuo sapore. I love how you taste." His voice was deeper. Huskier. He sucked his finger into his mouth.

I whimpered and sat up, reaching for him.

Drio bit my bottom lip. "Spogliami. Undress me."

His shirt came off no problem, but I fumbled at his belt buckle as he sucked my tit in his mouth, rasping his teeth over my nipple.

Somehow, I managed to free his cock.

He fisted it in a slow stroke. "Who goes first?"

"How about together?" I scooted into the center of the bed.

Drio stretched over me in sixty-nine position. "Succhiami il cazzo."

That needed no translation. I sucked him into my mouth.

Drio licked and sucked my clit, the cool air washing over my sticky skin. He thrust two fingers inside me, fucking me in agonizing leisureliness.

It was a seduction in slow motion.

Sweat dripped down my breasts and something inside me clenched, a deep ache that only Drio could ease. I licked the salt on the head of his dick, Drio humming in response, vibrating against my clit that swelled, a hot heat coiling inside me.

My hips began to buck and I rocked against his tongue, riding his fingers, his stubble rasping against my inner thighs.

Drio rolled away from me and yanked the drawer on the bedside table open. "Not yet. Not until I've fucked you. I want you to come when I'm inside you. Sì?"

"Yes."

He rolled the condom on and stood at the edge of the bed, jerking me toward him by my hips. His abs rippled, shadows playing across his well-defined torso. "Wrap your legs around me."

I was ready for hard and fast, dirty Italian words falling from his lips.

He glided inside me, his body pressed to mine and worshipped me with sweet kisses and murmured endearments. Drio spun me in desire; I'd never been so cherished. This wasn't fucking, it was making love.

A startled cry burst out of me, my orgasm rocketing through me. I caught his face in my hands and pressed a long, lingering kiss to him.

"Turn over," he growled. "Get on your knees."

I bit my lip. "Really? From behind? We don't–okay, never mind."

"Leonie." His eyes locked on mine, the depth of his feeling for me reflected in them and laid bare for my taking. "We're solid. I just want you every way imaginable." He kissed me hungrily and lust speared through me.

I flipped onto all fours.

"Wider." He nudged my legs further apart and put my hand on my clit.

"Drio, I've got nothing left."

"You sure?" He played with me.

My hips began to rock, another orgasm building inside me. I pushed back against him, resting my head against the bed as Drio thrust into me. My body shook in delicious tremors, my gaze unfocused. I was lost to everything except this claiming, this bonding.

Maybe he didn't need to look at me, but I needed to look at him. I twisted to see him over my shoulder, and the smile that lit up his face was brighter than the noon sun.

He groaned, shuddering, his orgasm pushing me over the edge. I came with a sharp cry.

Mate. The voice was my goblin's... and mine. I rolled out from under him, tapping a finger against my lips.

"Madonna mia. Woman, you're insatiable. Give me five minutes to recharge."

I pushed him playfully. "Get over yourself."

"Then what?"

"Okay, so, uh, how do you feel about mating rituals?" I mumbled, eyes glued to the comforter cover like there would be a test on the abstract pattern. "Goblin ones."

Drio propped himself up on one elbow, confused. "Che cosa?"

For a moment, I debated not telling him. But we were a team now, me and my goblin, and to deny her this would be me turning my back on us both. I steeled myself and spit it out.

"My redcap, uh, recognized you as her mate."

His eyes widened and a boyish wonder stole over his face briefly, as if he'd thought there was nothing in this world he hadn't seen and the sheer impossibility of this newness delighted him. Then, as quickly as it had come, it was replaced with that familiar, insufferable smirk. "Oh, she did, did she? What about you?"

I snarled. "A little less with every passing second."

His smirk got wider. "You gonna make an honest man out of me?"

"We're about twenty years too late on that score."

"Leonie…"

"It's not flowers and a proposal, Drio." I threw up my hands. "We have to spill our blood to prove that the other person is more important than blood, and then I have to anoint you in jewels, okay? Happy?"

That killed the smirk. He rubbed the back of his neck, his bottom lip caught between his teeth.

"Forget it." I turned over.

He leaned over me, his face in mine. "What if I do it wrong?"

"That's what you're worried about?"

He speared me with an "obviously" look. "I don't need a goblin side to know you're it for me, but rituals are important, and I don't want to blow this."

Neither did I. Almost losing Drio had forced me to recognize what he meant to me. If I could stop hiding from my demon self, I could stop hiding from my feelings. I trusted him and I wanted him. Only him.

A few minutes later, we sat still naked on my bed. I'd spread a hand towel over the mattress on which I'd placed a sterilized switchblade and a blue cloth pouch.

I picked up the knife, feeling its heft and weight. "Goblins don't say anything when they do this because they understand the significance, but I'd like to, if that's okay."

Drio nodded. "Of course."

"I feel like the monster in the fairy tale. No," I added, heading off his protest, "I don't mean it in a bad way. Well, not anymore. I thought that because of what I was I'd never find my prince or princess, because if I trusted any normal person with the truth, they'd run screaming. Then I met you."

Drio laughed. "Grazie."

"But it's true. Nava and Rohan fit because they both bring each other into the light, but you and I live half in darkness. We both understand that about the other person."

"I'm your monster?"

"No, Drio. You're my monster king." I slashed my palm, letting the blood drip onto the hand towel. There was no surge of blood lust, no fight from my goblin. Just a contentedness that permeated my entire being. "You, Drio Rossi, are more precious to me than blood. Mon cher amour, I love you with all my heart."

I held the knife out to him but he didn't take it right away and I couldn't decipher his expression. When he finally took the blade from me and spoke, his voice was hoarse.

"I am honored to be the person who gets to know the real you, because you're radiant. I've always had this darkness in me and I either lied about it to myself or let it define me. I lived in these extremes, but with you I don't have to. You're my monster."

I mean, sure, I'd started that analogy, but I would have accepted "you're the gorgeous love of my life," as well. "Thanks?"

Drio grinned at me, full of wild chaos and sharp edges. "I give you my crazy, shadow-filled heart because only another monster is fierce enough and strong enough to keep it safe. My monster queen who is also the most beautiful woman in the world. Every moment I have with you is going to be glorious. You are more precious to me than blood, Leonie Hendricks, and I love you with all my heart."

That was acceptable. I did a little wriggly dance.

He slashed his palm. His blood dripped onto the towel, mingling with mine. A deep certainty settled into my bones.

"Now, you gonna bling me up?" he said.

I dumped the contents of the pouch out: diamond hoop earrings, a long string of pearls, and two ruby rings, which I placed in his hands. "I give these to you because I hold you above my most prized treasures. Now you refuse them to prove your love for me is beyond jewels."

Drio hung the earrings off his ears, wrapped the pearls around his neck, and then slid the rings onto his pinky fingers, which was the only place they fit. "I dunno." He waggled his fingers by his face. "They bring out the green in my eyes."

He looked ridiculous, but also kind of awesome, sitting there naked and confident, adorned in my jewels.

"Seriously, give them back." My fingers twitched.

He cocked an eyebrow. "But I look so pretty."

I tackled him and wrenched the jewelry off, pressing the items securely to my chest.

"You're cooing to them," he said.

I froze. "Am not."

He pressed his lips together but a snort of laughter escaped him.

I swatted him. "Shut up."

"Make me." His eyes heated and since I never met a naked Drio dare I planned on resisting, I tackled him again.

Eventually we moved into my bathroom where Drio filled the tub and I slid into the hot water, leaning back against him and running my foot over his shin. "I'm ready to have dinner with your parents if you survive Harry."

Drio nibbled on the hollow of my neck and I squirmed, ticklish. "Could I just bleed some more?" he said.

"Coward."

"I hurt you," Drio said. "He must hate me."

"You're not his favorite person." I wrapped his arms around me. "But Harry basically starts off hating everyone unless you're exceptional, like me." I snickered. "See how much you two have in common?"

Drio growled against my neck.

"Don't worry, you'll win him over." I paused. "How do you feel about the P.I. business? Harry wants to retire sooner rather than later."

He was quiet for so long that I got fidgety.

Yikes. I'd asked him to be my mate and my business partner all in the same night. Maybe it was too much at once? Had Drio seen the creepy cat watercolors? I struggled to remember.

186

"Never mind," I said. "I really am okay with taking it slow. You have your Rasha stuff and—"

"Leonie."

I twisted around to face him and he kissed me, hot and deep.

"Is that a yes?" I said when we came up for air.

"It's a hell yes. We'll be the demon-Rasha Watson and Holmes," he said.

"I'm Holmes," we said in unison.

"We'll work on it." I relaxed against him. "You know, we only got about two hours together the night you sang to me."

"Sort of an entire night if we count Limbo as a date." He sucked on the sensitive skin at the base of my throat.

"Tracking and killing a demon was a date?" I said.

"I did feed you beforehand."

"Oh, then it totally counts. How long do you think we have until the next threat to our very existence?" I tilted my head back to look at him.

"We're good for a week, at least."

I cocked an eyebrow at him.

He shrugged. "A solid twenty-four hours?"

"Better make it count," I said and reached for him.

THANK you for reading LEONIE HENDRICKS: DEMON P.I.

Haven't read Nava's story yet? Go back to the beginning with THE UNLIKEABLE DEMON HUNTER.

An all-male brotherhood hunts demonic foes. But their biggest threat could be a foul-mouthed, romance-impaired heroine who's gonna show these boys a thing or two about how to really slay a monster...

OR dive into my snarky supernatural detective series: BLOOD & ASH (THE JEZEBEL FILES BOOK 1)

Cold-blooded kidnappers. Long-lost magic. When things get serious, she goes full Sherlock.

Ashira Cohen takes pride in being the only female private investigator in Vancouver. With her skills, her missing persons case should be a piece of cake.

She wasn't counting on getting bashed in the skull, revealing a hidden tattoo and supernatural powers she shouldn't possess.

Or the bitter icing on top: a spree of abductions and terrifying ghostly creatures on a deadly bender.

And don't even get her started on the golems.

Reluctantly partnered with her long-time nemesis Levi, the infuriating leader of the magic community, Ash resolves to keep her focus on the clue trail and off their sexual tension because WTF is up with that?

But with a mastermind organization pulling strings from the shadows and Levi's arrogance driving her to pick out his body bag, can Ash rescue the captives and uncover the truth or will the next blood spilled be her own?

Every time a reader leaves a review, an author gets ... a glass of wine. (You thought I was going to say "wings," didn't you? We're authors, not angels, but *you'll* get heavenly karma for your good deed.) Please leave yours on your favorite book site.

Turn the page for an excerpt from *Blood & Ash* ...

EXCERPT FROM BLOOD & ASH

There was nothing like sitting in a shitty car with a broken heater covertly filming a teenager for cash to make me question my life choices.

My target, Charlotte Rose Scott, had taffy blonde hair, big blue eyes, and a manic enthusiasm that made me want to slip her an Ambien.

Not that I'd waste one on a child.

Her can-do spirit was currently being applied to a bit of breaking and entering. The sixteen-year-old had tried every point of entry on the ground floor of this weathered Craftsman house that was thirty-two blocks and worlds away from her own home. She'd graduated from tugging on the windows' security bars to wobbling her way up a bare trellis to the second-story balcony.

Good to know all those gymnastics and dance classes of hers had a practical application. It was so hard to make it in the arts, but crime was always a growth industry.

I slapped another memory card into my Handycam, absently rubbing my right thigh. I'd been sitting out here in the damp cold for too long, exacerbating the dull ache from the rods holding my femur together, so I grabbed the Costco-sized bottle of Tylenol that I'd tossed on the passenger seat and dry-swallowed a couple of pills.

She wrenched on the sliding door handle and I winced. Leave a few more fingerprints, why don't you? If it wouldn't completely compromise my case, I'd show her how to break in myself and put us both out of our misery.

I zoomed in, ready to capture C.R. living her best truth. Or better yet, get some answers. Come on, you little adolescent fiend. Why the uncharacteristic foray into robbery? You'd even blown off piano lessons for this and you thrived in your overscheduled teenage existence.

What was I missing?

Denied entry, she shimmied back down the trellis to run at the solid back door. When she bounced off it with a yelp, only one of us was surprised.

Spare me from amateurs.

I dug my buzzing phone out of my hip pocket. My best friend and part-time employee, Priya Khatri, had come through with the land title search on this property. I frowned at the text, trying to place the homeowner's name. Oh, fuck balls. I wasn't being paid to save Charlotte Rose from making a really stupid mistake.

This was not my problem.

Charlotte Rose rubbed her elbow, red from where she'd smacked into the door, and bit her lip, eyes watery.

Grumbling, I turned off the camera and got out of Moriarty, also known as my car, using both hands to swing my poor stiff leg onto the concrete. Tucking my fingers into the armpits of my battered leather jacket, my breath misting the air, I limped over to the tiny backyard of the crime spree in progress.

"Yo, Cat Burglar Barbie," I called out. "The jig is up!"

She froze for a second and then vanished into thin air.

I blinked, gaping at the empty space. "Charlotte Rose Scott, you get your butt back here this second and explain yourself, because you are not supposed to have magic!"

I'd done my due diligence before taking this case. Verified that she was a Mundane. No powers. Zero. Nada.

Except, apparently, she wasn't. And now, thanks to this unpleasant and unforeseen magical development, I was about to get royally fucked by House Pacifica.

Charlotte Rose flickered back into view, just a fist with her middle finger extended. I mean, impressive control on invisibility magic, but what a little shit.

"Leave her alone!" Another girl about the same age, who spoke with a light musical accent, raced into the backyard. Her worn denim jacket had "Fuck the patriarchy" written in thick silver marker across the back and her dyed black hair showed the ragged edges of someone who'd cut it herself.

Interesting choice for a co-conspirator.

When Victoria Scott had hired me to spy on her kid who'd been "acting cagey" and therefore obviously had some drug habit, she'd casually sported a linen dress that cost more than my much-needed car repairs. We'd spent a grand total of twenty minutes together, all of them in her vanilla-scented Williams Sonoma kitchen with its neatly shelved cookbooks–written by obscure foodies–whose spines weren't even cracked.

I'd bet anything that this wrong-side-of-the-tracks friend was not part of Victoria's bourgie starter-pack vision of the good life.

"Stand down," I told the new girl. "And if you know what's good for you, you'll tell Charlotte Rose to show herself."

The newcomer called up a gust of wind and flung it at me.

I flew backwards, stumbling over a plastic Adirondack chair, and cracked my skull on the corner of the house so hard that I saw stars. My leg buckled briefly as I bounced off the wooden siding and staggered forward, choking on a hot rush of bile. Gritting my teeth, I touched a finger to the back of my head and came away with a wet, red smear.

Awesome. A pissy air elemental. Just what my day needed.

I found the tiny box stashed in my jacket pocket and pushed its single button. It produced a high-frequency sound barely within hearing range that made the newbie double over and caused Charlotte Rose to become visible once more, clapping her hands over her ears and moaning in pain.

I braced a hand against the bricks to combat my own dizziness. This admittedly illegal sonic weapon should not have affected me this way because I'd built up a tolerance.

Why, hel-*lo* concussion. On the upside, however lackluster the case had been to solve intellectually, I *had* solved it so at least I'd get paid. With C.R.'s true nature revealed, billable hours took a back seat to getting this kid home safely before she ended up with a juvie record, so I powered through the nausea and slapped a pair of cuffs on these criminal toddlers before they could regroup.

I dialed a number on my phone.

"It's Ashira Cohen," I said, when Victoria answered. "Tell your daughter she has permission to get in my car."

Victoria stuttered out protests that she had no idea who I was or what I was talking about, but I cut her off with an exasperated huff. Not this again. Everyone thought they were so clever denying they'd hired a P.I. when things got tough. It didn't work that way.

"Enough bullshit. If you want help getting out of the mess you've landed in with your unregistered Nefesh kid, then give the all-clear for me to drive her home."

Victoria answered with a meek "okay." Damn straight, you better comply.

Nowadays, most people preferred to hire private investigators who had magic, wanting the extra abilities that Nefesh brought to the table. I was the only female P.I. in town, very much outside the boys' club of this industry, and a Mundane to boot. I'd worked my ass off to carve out a niche for myself and Victoria wasn't going to jeopardize that.

I passed the phone to Charlotte Rose, who listened to her mother without comment, glaring at me the entire time. I held that gaze and raised her glower with an arched eyebrow. Snotty teens were the worst. I'd know.

C.R. handed me the cell and linked hands with her friend, the two of them edging closer together.

"I have rights," the second girl howled, shaking the cuffs as if trying to blow them off.

"Nope," I said. "You lost them under Statue 7.5, 'demonstrating exceeding stupidity.' And save your energy. Those puppies suppress magic."

"You're not a cop," she countered. "You'd have identified yourself. And if you had magic you'd have used it. That means, you're not Nefesh and you're not allowed to have shit like this. Or use it on me."

It's true, the cuffs were totally a "fell off the back of a van" purchase, but a woman did what she had to. Just because I wasn't allowed to work magic cases, that didn't preclude supposedly Mundane ones from going sideways–like this one had. "Yeah? How would you know?"

"Television," the girl said. "So what are you?"

I flashed her my P.I. license. "A real-life detective who knows what equipment she's allowed to have far better than you."

Charlotte Rose puffed out her chest. "I won't let her hurt you, Meryem."

"Aw. That's… deluded." I herded the girls to Moriarty, trying not to limp too badly. Never show those monsters weakness. Weirdly, I could still smell blood, as if it was gushing out of me like a waterfall. It wasn't even that bad, kind of earthy and rich. I touched the back of my head. There was some matted in my dark waves, but the bleeding itself had stopped.

Meryem refused to get into my fine vehicle, holding her wrist pointedly against her chest once I'd uncuffed her as though I'd caused permanent nerve damage. "You gonna kidnap me?"

What a drama queen. "Much as I hate to deprive myself of your stellar company, no."

"Then I can get myself home."

"Mer–" Charlotte Rose sighed. "Be safe, okay?" She leaned in and gave Meryem a quick kiss.

Meryem blushed, scraping one of her raggedy high tops along the ground.

Even I, with my cold, dead heart, found their coupledom adorable.

"Here." I fished out what was pretty close to my last forty bucks.

"Fuck you. I'm not a charity case," Meryem said.

Maybe not, but she was in a jean jacket and had to be freezing in the miserable March weather. No way she had a good home to go to, if any at all. However, she was also prickly and if I was too nice–generally not an accusation thrown my way–she'd bolt.

"Consider it compensation for pain and suffering." I shoved the bills at her.

They disappeared so fast into her pocket that I made a note to get this girl some help.

"Thanks," she said, her eyes flickering uncertainly up to mine.

"Get lost before I change my mind."

She squeezed C.R.'s hand and bolted.

I fumbled at the door handle because there seemed to be two of them, then sank gratefully into the driver's seat, taking a couple of steadying breaths before I leaned over to unlock the passenger door, knocking the Tylenol bottle onto the floor.

C.R. got into the car, keeping her distance.

Using the rag that I kept to defog the windshield since the heater didn't work, I wiped myself down because my hair was sweatily plastered to my neck. I ignored Charlotte Rose's grimace that came with huffy sound effects.

Once I was dry-ish and reality had stabilized enough to drive safely-ish, I patted Moriarty's dashboard twice and turned the key, whispering, "Who's a good boy?" and praying this wasn't the moment he died on me once and for all. Not like he hadn't faked his death more than once. But he started with only the mildest choke.

Neither C.R. nor I spoke for the first half of the ride.

"You going to out me?" she said.

I braked at a red light and glanced over at her. The world swung sideways and I gripped the steering wheel tight until my equilibrium was restored.

C.R.'s words were sneered but her pupils were slightly dilated.

I slowly faced forward so as not to jiggle my brain. "Contrary to popular belief and genetics, I have a moral compass. It's up to you to tell your mom about Meryem. So, why invisibility magic?"

"Mom used to play this game where she'd pull the blanket up over my eyes and say, 'Where's Charlotte Rose?' Apparently, I went nuts for it."

Uh-huh. Cute answer but there was more to it than that. While Nefesh were born with magic, the precise nature of it developed during childhood and was rooted in psychological primal drives.

The light turned green and I hit the gas, wincing at Moriarty's jerky start. "And the attempted robbery?"

"I wasn't going to steal anything," she said hotly.

I let the silence grow.

It took her all of two blocks to break.

"It was my birth mother's place," she said. "I wanted to see..."

"What Darleen's life was like without you?"

Charlotte Rose shrugged, a mess of emotions playing across her face that she tried to hide under a sullen disinterest. Then it hit her. "You knew? Is that why you stopped me?"

I made a smooth left. "Figured you didn't want your big reunion to be from juvie."

She crossed her arms and stared straight ahead.

Thankfully, it was a short drive from there, because by the

time we pulled up to her large Tudor home with its pricy S.U.V. parked in the driveway, my skin felt two sizes too small, and the world's worst itch had settled between my shoulder blades, exactly where I couldn't reach.

This time, I met Victoria in her living room, decorated with that faux rustic charm involving unpainted wood, a chunky stone fireplace wafting out the scent of pine, and cutesy large prints with sayings like "Laugh. Live. Breathe." that made me want to "Gag. Run. Drink."

Victoria greeted me in a purple bamboo yoga number that would have been very comfortable to move in, except I doubted she did classes in full makeup, her blonde-streaked hair twisted in a chignon and large diamonds flashing in her ears.

Inner peace through Tiffany's. Namaste, bitches.

"Charlotte Rose," Victoria said. "What's going on?"

"You hired her to spy on me?" C.R.'s glower at her mom should have incinerated her.

"I hired her because I was concerned that my daughter was a drug addict!" Victoria planted her hands on her hips and the two of them broke into a furious squabble.

I whistled loudly, pain flaring inside my skull. Eyes half-squinted shut, I massaged my temples. I could patch myself up with some aspirin and a good night's sleep. Nothing to fear. "Your mom was worried. Suspicious and over-paranoid but worried. Charlotte Rose is not on drugs. Fight it out later."

Victoria sat down on the sofa next to her daughter. "Then why has she been behaving this way?"

She'd hired me to get answers and I had them, but this was a delicate situation. "She was curious about her birth mother. It's natural and isn't any reflection on you."

Victoria plucked at her sleeve.

"Mom?" Charlotte Rose reached out for Victoria and I braced myself for her mother's hurt dismissal, but Victoria surprised me and took her daughter's hand.

"I wish you had come to me first but I understand. When

we adopted you, Darleen made it clear that if you wanted to meet her, she was open to it, but we need to do this properly, okay?"

"Okay."

Victoria smiled at me and stood up. "Thank you. If you'd care to send your invoice–"

"Sit. Down."

She dropped like a stone onto the cushions.

I perched on the edge of a scratchy wing chair, hoping my casually braced elbow on the back didn't look like the desperate support to remain upright that it was. "Victoria, I specifically asked you in our intake interview if you could think of any Nefesh connection that would prevent me from taking this assignment. I'm not legally allowed to handle cases involving magic."

The law was asinine, supposedly "designed to protect Mundanes like me." Right. Try more money in House coffers since all Nefesh paid taxes towards House resources and protection. But it was what it was and, if House Pacifica found out, I'd be brutally fined, because they took this very seriously. I was already existing by the skin of my teeth. This would ruin me.

"Magic?" Victoria said, and flushed a faint pink.

I stared at her until her shoulders slumped.

"Her birth mother was from a good Mundane family and there was no father listed on her birth certificate," Victoria said. "Nothing in the adoption showed that Charlotte Rose might be Nefesh through the birth father."

"Yeah, I'm aware of that part, since I investigated it thoroughly. However, you knew about Charlotte Rose and you kept it from me." I practically threw my arm out of its socket trying to get at the itch but it remained maddeningly out of reach. "Why me? You could have gone to a Nefesh P.I."

"I didn't want them to suspect. And you were cheaper," she admitted.

Slight as my accomplishments were, and my mother had

written a treatise on that, they were mine and I was super proud of them. Maybe I didn't have the interesting cases–yet–but a woman had to start somewhere and I was pulling this off on my terms. I'd get there.

I gave up on the itch and my anger. Victoria was not worth committing grievous bodily harm and losing everything. But man, it was close.

"Here's my advice," I said, catching myself before I did a slow slide off the chair and onto my ass. Okay, maybe my condition was a bit worse than presumed. "Take Charlotte Rose to House Pacifica and point her baby blues at them. Squeeze out a tear or two for good measure while you throw yourself on their mercy. Mom, you didn't know. Kid, you were scared to lose the love of your adoptive parents."

Charlotte Rose bit her lip, exchanging a glance with her mother.

"Hit the mark there, did I?" I said. "Let me guess. Dad has a few beliefs in common with the Untainted Party?" That explained the invisibility magic.

"How'd you know?" Victoria squeaked.

"I'm well versed on those people. They're a pretty popular political affiliation around here."

"I can't tell him." Charlotte Rose looked genuinely scared.

I softened my tone. "You don't have a choice. If you don't do it by tomorrow, I'll have to because all people with magic must be registered with the House in their region. A fact you damn well know. But since it'll be worse if I'm involved…" Mainly, for me. "It's in your best interests to keep me out of it and pile on the remorse."

"This feels really unsavory," Victoria said. "There has to be another way."

My dad's voice rang out loud and clear in my head. *There are two types of people in this world, Ash, my girl. Those who are marks and those who aren't.*

It had only taken me one harsh lesson to swear I'd never

make that mistake again. Victoria had tried to play me. Operative word being "tried."

"There isn't," I said. "Your kid is currently a Rogue. Fix it."

Charlotte Rose surged up like a fury of Greek myth. "I'm not registering with the House. They experiment on people."

Her voice hurt my ears. It was too loud, too grating.

"While I'm happy to think the worst of Levi Montefiore and House Pacifica..." I dabbed at the sweat on my brow. "They aren't running some mad scientist lab. They're legit, annoyingly so, and believe me, it's much worse to be on their bad side than on the same team."

My words sounded funny, all long and drawn out. Fuck. I was going to have to brave a hospital. Warning Victoria again to contact House Pacifica and reminding her that late payment on my bill was subject to interest, I made my excuses and stumbled out to Moriarty, whose headlights seemed to smirk evilly at me.

The drive to the closest Emergency Room was a blur. I pulled up to the entrance, tossed my keys at the attitude-laden valet in the fireman costume who totally wasn't getting a tip, lurched inside, and collapsed, unconscious.

GET A FREE DOWNLOAD

If you enjoyed this book, then how about some free short stories set in this world? Demons and sexytimes, galore! There are mild spoilers in each one, so it's best to enjoy them in the proper reading order of the Nava Katz series.

Go to: http://www.deborahwilde.com/subscribe

If you only want to be alerted to new releases then follow me on BookBub: https://www.bookbub.com/authors/deborah-wilde

1) Slay: Rohan's POV (Book 1.5)

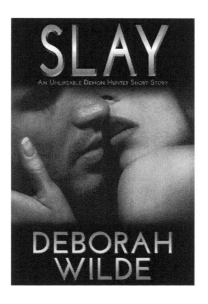

2) Crush: Drio's POV (Book 2.5)

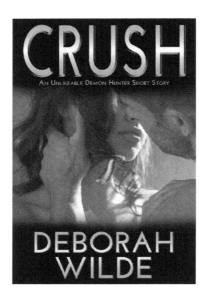

3) Seize: Rohan's POV (Book 3.5)

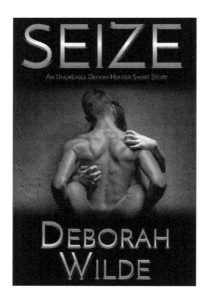

4) Lick: Ari's POV (Book 4.5 - m/m romance)

LICK

AN UNLIKEABLE DEMON HUNTER SHORT STORY

DEBORAH
WILDE

ACKNOWLEDGMENTS

Thank you to all my Wilde Ones who kept harassing me (uh, I mean nicely asking) for Leo's spin-off. *grin* Truly, if it weren't for you all, this story would never have been written.

And as always, thank you to my editor Alex Yuschik, who is the best, most insightful person to work with and also awesome as a cheerleader. I consider it quite the coup that mere weeks after wrapping up Nava's series, I made you nostalgic for all those characters with this book.

ABOUT THE AUTHOR

I'm Deborah (pronounced deb-O-rah) and I write sexy, funny, urban fantasy.

I decided at an early age to live life like it was a movie, as befitted a three-syllable girl. Mine features exotic locales, an eclectic soundtrack, and a glittering cast—except for those two guys left on the cutting room floor. Secret supernatural societies may be involved.

They say you should write what you know, which is why I shamelessly plagiarize my life to write about witty, smart women who kick ass, stand toe-to-toe against infuriating alphas, and execute any bad decisions in indomitable style.

"It takes a bad girl to fight evil. Go Wilde."

www.deborahwilde.com